Tricked

Also from Rebecca Zanetti

SCORPIUS SYNDROME SERIES
Scorpius Rising
Mercury Striking
Shadow Falling
Justice Ascending (January 27, 2017)

DARK PROTECTORS
Fated
Claimed
Tempted
Hunted
Consumed
Provoked
Twisted
Shadowed
Tamed
Marked
Teased
Tricked
Tangled

REALM ENFORCERS
Wicked Ride
Wicked Edge
Wicked Burn
Wicked Kiss (July 4, 2017)
Wicked Bite (August 1, 2017)

SIN BROTHERS
Forgotten Sins
Sweet Revenge
Blind Faith
Total Surrender

BLOOD BROTHERS
Deadly Silence
Lethal Lies
Twisted Truths

Tricked

A Dark Protectors Novella

By Rebecca Zanetti

1001 Dark Nights

EVIL EYE
CONCEPTS

Tricked
A Dark Protectors Novella
By Rebecca Zanetti

Copyright 2016 Rebecca Zanetti
ISBN: 978-1-942299-43-1

Foreword: Copyright 2014 M. J. Rose

Published by Evil Eye Concepts, Incorporated

Acknowledgments from the Author

I am truly thrilled to be included with the amazing authors in the 1001 Dark Nights group! A huge shout out thanks to Liz Berry, my very good friend who also is a brilliant businesswoman. Thank you also to MJ Rose, Kimberly Guidroz, and Pam Jamison for their dedication and awesome insights. A heartfelt thanks goes to Jillian Stein, the most amazing social media manager in the world. Thanks also to Asha Hossain, who creates absolutely fantastic book covers.

As always, a lot of love and a huge thank you goes to Big Tone, Gabe and Karly, my amazing family who is so supportive.

Finally, thank you to Rebecca's Rebels, my street team, who have been so generous with their time and friendship. Thank you to Minga Portillo for her excellent leadership of the team. And last, but not least, thank you to all of my readers who spend time with my characters.

~ RAZ

Sign up for the 1001 Dark Nights Newsletter
and be entered to win a Tiffany Key necklace.

There's a contest every month!

Go to www.1001DarkNights.com to subscribe.

As a bonus, all subscribers will receive a free
1001 Dark Nights story
The First Night
by Lexi Blake & M.J. Rose

One Thousand and One Dark Nights

Once upon a time, in the future…

I was a student fascinated with stories and learning.
I studied philosophy, poetry, history, the occult, and
the art and science of love and magic. I had a vast
library at my father's home and collected thousands
of volumes of fantastic tales.

I learned all about ancient races and bygone
times. About myths and legends and dreams of all
people through the millennium. And the more I read
the stronger my imagination grew until I discovered
that I was able to travel into the stories… to actually
become part of them.

I wish I could say that I listened to my teacher
and respected my gift, as I ought to have. If I had, I
would not be telling you this tale now.
But I was foolhardy and confused, showing off
with bravery.

One afternoon, curious about the myth of the
Arabian Nights, I traveled back to ancient Persia to
see for myself if it was true that every day Shahryar
(Persian: شهریار, "king") married a new virgin, and then
sent yesterday's wife to be beheaded. It was written
and I had read, that by the time he met Scheherazade,
the vizier's daughter, he'd killed one thousand
women.

Something went wrong with my efforts. I arrived
in the midst of the story and somehow exchanged
places with Scheherazade — a phenomena that had
never occurred before and that still to this day, I
cannot explain.

*Now I am trapped in that ancient past. I have
taken on Scheherazade's life and the only way I can
protect myself and stay alive is to do what she did to
protect herself and stay alive.*

*Every night the King calls for me and listens as I spin tales.
And when the evening ends and dawn breaks, I stop at a
point that leaves him breathless and yearning for more.
And so the King spares my life for one more day, so that
he might hear the rest of my dark tale.*

*As soon as I finish a story... I begin a new
one... like the one that you, dear reader, have before
you now.*

Chapter 1

Ronni Alexander settled back into the cushiony sofa in her small loft outside of New York City and forced her expression into calm lines. "Thank you for the ride home." Yeah, she'd meant the words as a dismissal.

Apparently Jared Reese didn't know how to take a hint. "You're more than welcome." His voice was husky to the point of being gritty and settled along her skin like it wanted to stay. He stood in the center of her living room, making the area seem so much smaller than it normally appeared. He was the tallest, broadest, and most dangerous person she'd ever invited into her home, and the jewel colors around him only emphasized his darkness.

Black hair, black eyes, black leather jacket. But it wasn't just the absence of color. It was the look in those eyes and the tension in that tight body.

She cleared her throat and moved to stand.

He waved her back down. "I'm not leaving until we discuss my offer." He shrugged out of his jacket.

The play of muscle, raw and powerful, through his faded T-shirt caught her attention. She shook her head. "Not now. I'll call you."

His full lips twitched, and a sparkle lightened those eyes just enough to make them gleam like a predator hunting at night. "The offer is only good for the next hour or so." He sat and the very faded denim across his thighs stretched. The man overwhelmed the oversized reading chair. "Not that you have much time left."

She swallowed. "Can you tell how long?"

"No, but I can hear your heart beating with a stutter way too slowly." He lowered his chin and studied her, his rugged face set in strong lines. "Even your lips are blue from lack of oxygen, Veronica."

Only her grandmother back in Colombia used her full name—and usually when Ronni was in trouble. But at the moment, she had more important things to concentrate on while her brain still worked. If she died, she'd fail once again. Just like her father had said she would. She shook her head, banishing thoughts of her crappy childhood and the fact that he'd never see what she'd become, considering he'd died years ago. "Show me again," she said softly, turning her attention back to the man inside her apartment.

Jared tilted his head to the side. "You have the oddest fascination, lady."

She nodded. "Probably."

He sighed and opened his mouth, allowing razor-sharp fangs to slide down.

She shivered, her gaze caught. "Amazing."

He rolled his eyes, and the fangs disappeared. "Not really."

Yes, really. Vampires existed. As in really, really, really existed. She rubbed her legs, trying to warm her freezing hands. "How don't we humans know about you?"

"Don't want you to," he said, surveying the small apartment decorated with pumpkins, ghouls, and ghosts. "You're a couple of seasons behind with the decor."

Yeah, she should probably have her tree up. Christmas would arrive in about two weeks. "I know. I became ill around Halloween and haven't taken the time to redecorate. No energy, to be honest. However, I love Halloween, so these decorations make me feel happy." Her hands trembled. Heaviness settled on her shoulders, weakening her arms. She blinked and tried to keep her eyes open. "Our legends aren't true, then. I mean, you can go into sunlight, right?"

"Yep."

She tried to sit up straighter. "What if I staked you in the heart?"

"You'd just piss me off," he said evenly.

Even though it wasn't a threat, she caught an undercurrent of truth in the statement. Pissing him off would probably be a bad idea.

"What can kill you?"

"Beheading." He glanced at the snow falling outside the window, energy flowing from him. "I think full burning might work, but it'd have to be to the point of ashes, you know?"

"Of course," she said with just a hint of bewilderment.

"Make a decision, Veronica." His focus returned absolutely to her, power in his eyes and strength in every movement. How was he even real?

She tried to face him when all her defenses were just gone. "I have more questions."

"Of course you do," he muttered, wiping a hand across his eyes. "Fine. That's fair. Ask away."

What did one ask a vampire? What if she did accept his offer? "Do you have bags of blood in your refrigerator?"

He blinked. "God, no. Why?"

Oh, crap. So he fed on humans. Would he want to feed on her? "You want to ah, mate me, so you have blood?"

His brows drew down. "Huh?"

A shiver racked her.

"Sweetheart." He stood and grabbed a blanket off the sofa to wrap around her. "You're weakening."

She'd been weakening for about two months. Her heart hitched at his kindness. His protection. What would it be like to truly be with a man like him? "That's what happens when your heart slowly dies. Well, when a human heart dies. Do you have a heart?"

"Yes." He sat back down, his elbows on his knees, his body leaning toward her. "Our anatomy is just like yours, except we have more chromosomal pairs that make us essentially immortal. Human to vampire is a lot like comparing plants to humans—on a chromosomal level."

Fascinating and oh so very tempting. "Do you hunt humans for blood?"

His expression cleared. "Oh. I get it. No. We make our own blood and don't need yours. Well, we do bite during battle or sex, but that's more of survival and choice."

Sex. Heat bloomed into her face. "Legends are really wrong."

"Yep." He rubbed his whiskered chin.

How had she missed such information? Leave it to Olly to

discover the truth. "Will Olivia become a vampire?"

"No. Your friend and my brother plan to mate. Her chromosomal pairs will duplicate until she's almost immortal, but that's the only change." He leaned forward even more, and his masculine scent settled all around her. "I'm offering you the same thing, Veronica. If we mate, you'll become immortal and you won't die from this disease."

It wasn't a disease. Yet it was going to kill her, without question. Probably within a week or so. What would immortality be like? Probably pretty freaking awesome. If nothing else, it'd give her time to hunt down the bastard who thought he'd killed her, finally proving her father wrong. She was strong, and she could survive in this world. Yet, she didn't know this man. "Why are you offering?" She truly didn't understand.

He shrugged. "Family is everything to us. My brother loves your best friend, and she's heartbroken that you're about to die. If you live, then maybe I'd see more of Chalton."

Was that a glimmer of sweetness revealed in the badass? He obviously loved his brother. Tough guys understood loyalty, now didn't they? As a psychologist, Ronni loved delving into motivations. "Olivia said that you and your brother haven't talked in a long time."

"We haven't, and I want to change that." He flattened a hand on his jeans. A big and broad hand. "It's only been a century, but even so. I've missed him."

A century? "How old are you?"

"Ah, I think about four hundred and twenty-seven?" He quirked his lip. "Maybe twenty-eight. Time runs together."

He looked thirty, tops. She tried to grasp the new reality and studied his face. Way too rough to be called handsome, the hard ridges and planes created a wild beauty that matched the glint in his eyes. Straight nose, high cheekbones, masculine mouth.

A predator harder to catch than the wind.

She shook her head. Now she was becoming poetic. Yep. She was near death. "You said earlier that mating is forever." She barely kept from stuttering on the word "mating."

"It is." He reached for her, enclosing her chilled hand in warmth.

Energy thrummed between them, heating her throughout. When was the last time she'd been warm? "But Olivia said it might not be?" What if the mating was just temporary? Ronni would take the immortality if it was that easy, wouldn't she?

Jared shook his head. "It's forever, Veronica. While there is a virus that has negated a mating bond well after one party has died, it hasn't been tried in two living mates, and it won't be in our case. Too dangerous, and I won't allow it."

Warning crept up her spine.

Every once in a while, his mask slipped. Oh, on the surface, he was calm and gentle…even reasonable.

Yet…a restless energy crackled from him. A force with strength she barely imagined but could sense. On a primitive level, she knew without question there was more to Jared Reese than he was letting her see. What exactly was a vampire?

He'd have her believe he was just another species.

So was the jaguar.

Even in her weakened state, her body hummed near him as if his primitive energy captured hers. "Since you're so old, I'll let the word 'allowed' pass. This time." It took all her strength, mental and physical, to meet his gaze without blinking.

"Ah." He didn't move an inch but somehow seemed bigger. Stronger. More focused. "It's good we're having this chat."

The entire world felt unsteady around her. "What do you want from me, Jared?"

It was the first time she'd used his name, and by the straightening of his body, he knew it. "Excuse me?"

"You're offering me life and immortality. What do you want from me?" Favors were never free, and she had to know the full facts before agreeing. The way he looked at her kept her pinned in place. She was so out of her depth with him. "There has to be something."

His expression revealed absolutely nothing. "All right. Here it is. Mating you gets me three things I want. One, I get to see more of my brother. Two, I get my mother and all other relatives off my back about finding a mate. Three, someday I get children."

She leaned back into the sofa, her breath heating. "From me."

His cheek creased. "Yeah. From you."

So this was more than a one-night deal. "Wait a minute."

He held up a hand. "I don't mean tomorrow or even during this century. Five hundred years from now would be fine. But someday, I do want a family. As my mate, you're pretty much the only one who can give me sons."

"Or daughters," she said almost automatically, her mind spinning.

"No." He smiled now, transforming his face into raw beauty. "Vampires are male only. We'd have sons."

Sons. Big, strong, dark little boys. Her damaged heart thumped. Strong and nearly immortal boys who she could adore forever. "What about love?" she asked, surprising herself.

"Even for humans, arranged marriages work out more than those founded by love," he said evenly. "I want an agreement and you get to live. Take the deal."

She came from a long line of passionate women, some still in Colombia, and others scattered across the world. Love meant something to them and to her. "You've never been in love," she mused.

"Wrong." He tightened his hold on her hand. "I did love a woman, a witch, and she mated somebody else two centuries ago."

A witch? Seriously? Ronnie jerked her head. "Witches exist?"

"Yep. Another species. They use quantum physics to alter matter."

Wow. Life was so different than she'd imagined. She'd find out more about witches later. How could any woman reject love from a man like this? The witch must be crazy. Even without love, an offer from a guy like Jared was tempting. He was sex and danger personified. "You think you won't find it again. You might."

He flipped his hand over and captured both of hers in a reassuring hold. "Nope. I'm not looking for love again, and that's just fine with me. I like the thought of our arrangement."

An arranged mating. She'd be giving up love but gaining life. A forever with Jared. Intrigue had her trying to concentrate. "I'm not ready to die," she whispered, her chest compressing.

"Then don't die."

It was so simple for him, but she could barely think straight. Not enough oxygen was reaching her brain, and she knew it. "I need to rest before I make a decision."

"Your head won't be any clearer than it is right now," Jared said, his face implacable.

"Okay." She tugged her hands free to dig them into her hair. "Say we mate. Olivia says it's sex with a bite and forever." Sex. With Jared.

With that body.

"Yes."

"Then what? You take off, and we meet up again in about five hundred years?" She tried to ignore her clamoring body and concentrate on the facts. To have kids. Yeah. That kind of thing could be scheduled, probably. Just think what she could accomplish in five centuries.

"Well, not exactly. I'd set you up with a nice place and a monthly allowance, and you can do what you want." He breathed out. "I'd visit periodically to see you and my family."

Humor burst through her. Had he really just used the word *allowance*? "You're kidding." She grinned.

"No."

She laughed, unable to help herself. "You want a mistress. Not a mate."

"No, I don't." He frowned, his entire face angled in one way or another.

Intriguing. She could spend an entire century just deciphering his expressions. "Sure. You keep me in style and show up for a good lay once in a while. How convenient."

His nostrils flared. "If we mate, we're the only people we can have sex with. If either of us tries to get intimate with somebody else, the mating allergy kicks in, and it totally sucks. Think the worse attack of poison ivy imaginable."

"Then there *are* requirements you want." The idea of sex with him shot a welcomed energy through her body to pulse in her erogenous zones. Yet she was no man's plaything, whether he saved her life or not. "I think you need to be a little clearer with your demands here."

"I thought it was obvious."

Truth be told, he did seem a little surprised by her response. She took a deep breath. "Here's the deal. I want to live."

"Good." His expression smoothed out.

"But I'm not willing to be a mistress." God, she wanted to live. To see the future. To have children. "I understand we can only have sex with each other, and I do like sex." At least she'd used to like it. "I'm not a sure thing. Meaning, you have no rights to me."

He studied her, energy radiating from him and brushing along her flesh. "First of all, no woman is ever a sure thing. Even during my time as a pirate on the high seas, I never forced a woman. Any and every time is your choice, and I would never force you. Ever."

Her chest settled. "Good. We're on the same page. And second?"

He leaned in, his nose nearly touching hers. "Second of all, if we mate, I have every right to you. Don't you ever forget it."

Chapter 2

Jared made sure he had the brunette's attention, giving her the full truth. Oh, he'd never force her, but mating came with obligations and responsibilities. Mainly, her life became his to protect.

Why did modern women think they were invincible?

Somehow, he wasn't getting his point across. It seemed as if she thought they'd mate and he'd go on his merry way and out of her life. While he didn't want a traditional mating or love, he also didn't want to be cast out into the cold. Who would take care of her?

Her bourbon-colored eyes darkened. Challenge and defiance filled them. A light pink brushed across her bronze skin. For the first time, he could see the woman she'd been before becoming ill.

Something awoke inside him. Power pulsed through his veins in an unconscious beat, and his lungs heated. His cock perked. No. Definitely...no. This was a fragile human, and he needed to remember that fact.

Forever.

He blinked away the image of who she could become and concentrated on the blue tinge to her lips and the frightening breakable bones beneath her smooth skin. "Do you have anybody to protect you?" he asked, wondering where her family was.

"Yeah. Me." She crossed her arms.

His breath sped up. "How about you lose the attitude and we talk?" Before he lost every one of his good intentions and kissed the chin she now jutted out. There was also a fullness to her mouth that made his ache to taste.

She swallowed. "I'm fine with talking, but you should check your own attitude."

His lips twitched. God, she was cute—spitting at him like a kitten hissing at a panther. "I'll ask again. Do you have family?"

"Just Olivia, whom I've known since preschool," Ronni said, her eyes clouding. "I lost my parents when I was twenty in a small plane wreck. No siblings, no other family." She hunched into herself and yet kept her head up.

Strong. The woman had a strength he hadn't noticed. "I'm sorry."

She nodded. "You?"

"Mother and two brothers," he said. "You met my entire family earlier today."

They'd had a little problem to deal with, and Ronni had been present to help. Then he'd offered to mate her after discovering her illness, and here they were.

She cleared her throat. "I'm not the right woman for you."

No. The right woman had followed duty, out of obedience, and mated somebody else. "You could be," he said softly.

"I'm not the type to belong to somebody, Jared."

Yet she would belong to him if they mated. "I don't think you're a handbag or a pair of shoes." Maybe the deflection would work.

"Right."

Nope. Didn't work. "Listen. I'm not human, and mating isn't a human experience." He searched for an explanation she'd understand. "It's permanent on a baser level."

She frowned. "You're not a man."

"No. I'm a male." Maybe that distinction would help her.

"Does mating hurt?" she asked softly.

The woman's thoughts bounced around quicker than a volleyball in a contested match. "The mating happens during sex, and I imagine the bite hurts a little." He kept his voice reassuring. Was the woman strong enough for sex? Even if he kept as gentle as possible, he might harm her. But what was the alternative? Temporary pain seemed better than her ultimate death, which would happen soon. "I'll try not to hurt you."

"I'm not afraid of pain. Just wanted to be prepared." She clutched the blanket closer around herself. "If I accept your offer."

It was already a done deal. He could see it in her eyes. "All right."

"You've been honest with me, and I want to be as transparent." She took in a deep breath and slowly let it out. "I don't want to die, and I would like immortality. Who wouldn't?"

"Agreed." Where was she going with this?

"You need to know who I am." She picked at a loose thread on the blanket. "Your vision of a woman waiting around for you and being supported by you isn't me. I usually can take care of myself, and I'm not going to change that."

"I imagine we'll have a bit of a disagreement, then," he said, enjoying the color sliding into her face. Finally. "How about we get you healthy and then take it from there?" His veins lit with heat. Anticipation?

"That's fair." Her jaw tightened visibly. "Once I am healthy, you need to know that I'm going to look into that virus that negates a mating bond."

He stilled. Hell. It was a bit insulting how little she wanted to be mated to him. In some circles, he was a catch. Even so, the virus was untested in a situation like theirs and would no doubt be dangerous. "No," he said very softly.

"Think you can stop me?" she said just as softly.

"Yes." Yep. That was anticipation.

She barely lifted a small shoulder. "Maybe...maybe not. Our cards are on the proverbial table. You still want to do this?"

More than ever. "I do."

"Okay." She glanced down, and more color tinged her cheeks. "I've never had a one-night stand."

"I have." Hell. He'd had plenty. "Though this isn't a one-night stand."

"We'll see." She looked back up. Delicate blue lines ran through the dark circles under her eyes. She was fading fast.

His chest settled. This was going to happen. "All right." He crossed to sit next to her, lifting her carefully onto his lap. Her butt hit his thighs, and he enfolded her almost too easily. Man, she was small. "Let's get you ready."

She sputtered and plastered one hand against his chest. "Don't need foreplay."

He stilled. A laugh rumbled up from his chest. He truly enjoyed how her mind worked. "Don't knock it until you've tried it." His fangs flashed low. "But I was talking about something else." Keeping her in place, he slashed into his wrist and then lifted it to her mouth. "Drink."

She plastered herself against his chest, trying to avoid his blood. "What the hell?"

Shit. He should've explained. "Our blood has some healing properties. Take a little, and it'll give you strength for the night."

She turned and looked into his face. "Seriously?"

"Yeah." He'd forgotten humans didn't like blood. "You'll feel better for a short time."

Something leaped into her eyes. A light. "What if I just drink a lot of your blood? Will that fix my heart?"

The woman really didn't want to mate him. "No." He gentled his voice to soften the truth. "Without being my mate, if you take too much blood, it'll kill you. You'd need a deadly dose to even temporarily fix your heart. It's impossible." He would've offered that in the first place, had there been a chance.

Her brow furrowed.

Whoa. She was thinking of taking the chance.

He shook his head. "Won't work. I promise." No way would he be responsible for killing her. For now, he could give her a small taste of immortality. "Now, drink," he whispered, holding his wrist to her mouth.

She kept her gaze on his and leaned in, swiping her tongue across his wrist.

Everything inside him seized. Fire roared through his chest, burned him throughout, and landed hard in his balls. He breathed out, shocked when there wasn't steam. "Again," he said, his voice guttural.

She blinked and wiggled on his suddenly rock-hard dick. Her eyes widened.

His narrowed. Pain pounded into his groin in a need so fierce he could barely breathe. His fangs lowered and pricked the inside of his mouth. His lip peeled back.

Her eyes widened.

Control. Fucking control. He slid his fangs home and forcibly calmed his entire body. Except his cock. That didn't calm. "Now," he said.

She looked up, fear in her eyes.

"I won't hurt you," he said.

The fear dissipated, leaving something else. Need. Definite need. Her lids half-lowered. She grasped his hand and pressed his wrist to her mouth, taking a deep swallow of his blood. She hummed in pure pleasure. Her eyes closed, and she tried for more.

"No." He pulled away, holding her still when she tried to follow his wrist. "Too much will hurt you."

She leaned back and licked a drop off her lips.

His pants tightened to the point of causing agony.

Color blew into her cheeks, and her eyes brightened. "God. It's amazing." Her voice had gone husky and low, and she might as well have whispered right across his bare cock.

His muscles tightened as he held himself in check.

She stretched her neck, her body moving against him. "I feel so good." Holding out her hand, she twisted her arm left and right. "Strong. Well, stronger than I just was." She rubbed her palm along his whiskers. "That's not all."

Yeah. He felt it, too. Attraction. So he turned her to straddle him, feeling her body warm several degrees. "Let me know if I go too fast."

She leaned in and settled her lips on his. "The first time I saw you, I thought wow. A real wow."

Her breath brushed his mouth, and he stiffened to remain in control. "Is that a fact?" he asked, waiting for her to make a move. The last thing he wanted to do was frighten her, and he couldn't tell how much stronger his blood had made her. If at all.

"Yes." She nibbled at his bottom lip.

Magma boiled through his blood. "When I first saw you, I thought your eyes were the prettiest color I'd ever seen," he said against her mouth. "Like a fine whiskey that has just caught the light."

She kissed him, and he could feel her smile. "That's sweet," she whispered.

Yeah. That was him. Sweet. Nobody in his entire life had called him that. "I don't want to rush you," he said.

She tunneled her hands through his hair and hummed. "But we're on a bit of a deadline?"

"Yeah." The slight tug of her fingers hazed red over his vision. "Don't know how long your extra strength will last." Probably not very long. And there could be repercussions to her damaged heart from his blood, so they had to mate and now. He stood, easily holding her to him. "Bedroom."

She wrapped her legs around his waist. "Um. Okay."

He swallowed and carried her through the small apartment and to the only doorway from the living room. Her bedroom was decorated in rich purples and blues…with scarlet accents. A room for passion.

Who was this woman? He'd have centuries to figure that out.

Careful not to jostle her, he set her on the bed.

Her gaze dropped, and her face flushed. Shyness all but rolled off her along with a hint of panic.

Hell. He crouched down until she faced him. "It's okay, baby."

She blinked. "This is weird. I mean, you're sexy as hell and anybody would want you, and I do. But I don't know you." She looked over his shoulder at the doorway. "Maybe we should get drunk."

The woman was adorable. He chuckled. "There's not enough booze in the city to really get me drunk, and I'm not sure your heart could take a sedative. How about I show you what I've learned in four centuries?"

Interest filtered through the embarrassment in those spectacular eyes. "You've got skills, huh?" A small smile played with her pink lips.

"Yeah." He wrapped a hand around her arm and drew her toward him, gently taking her mouth.

She sighed against him and returned his kiss—tentatively at first and then with more strength. Her hands flattened against his chest, and she moved into him even more. She suddenly coughed.

He leaned back. "Veronica?"

She shuddered and clasped a hand against her chest. The color deserted her face. "Um."

Shit. He jumped up and ripped his clothes off, grateful he was still hard from their play on the couch. "Hurry."

Her eyes widened, and she stood, her fingers fumbling with her shirt.

He could hear her heart slowing. "Sorry." Grabbing her shirt, he ripped it down the front.

Her chuckle was more of a wheeze.

He yanked off her jeans, gently finding her core. Wet. She was a little wet from earlier. Thank God. "Okay. This first time is going to be quick."

She nodded, her lips turning blue.

Damn it. She wasn't getting any oxygen to her face. Her heart was only stuttering its last minutes. He paused, grasping her hips. "Are you sure?"

"Yes," she whispered, her eyes clear. "I want to live, Jared."

Good enough. He laid her back and covered her. "I'm sorry."

She widened her thighs. "Hurry up," she wheezed.

He pressed his forehead to hers, willing her heart to keep beating. Slowly, as carefully as he could, he started to enter her. She was too fucking tight—and warm. He had to halt.

She dug her nails into his ass. "Hurry," she whispered.

Closing his eyes, he shoved inside her completely. She arched against him, pain on her hiss.

"I'm so sorry," he murmured.

Her eyelids fluttered open. "Whoa. You're huge," she said, a smile playing on her pale lips.

He coughed out a laugh. How could she joke right now? His heart warmed. So did his dick. She pulsed around him, tight and hot. Wet. Perfect. He slowly slid out to shove back in.

She blinked. "That feels...good." Her smile was weak but there. "Again."

He did as she said, setting up a good rhythm that was as gentle as he could be. She rocked against him, her ankles clasping at his back. Color slid into her face. "It's been a while," she said, wonder in her voice.

He could still feel her heart stuttering, so he reached between them and rubbed her clit. Her skin was unbelievably soft against his calloused fingers.

She arched against him again with a small cry, shutting her eyes. Part of him wanted to tell her to keep them open so he could watch her go over, but if she needed to keep them closed to get there, he'd let her.

This time.

Her breath caught, and her body stiffened. He rubbed harder. She dug her nails into his back and broke, her body undulating around his cock, even the waves somehow gentle.

Relief filled him. He pounded harder, sliding his fangs down.

Her eyes opened, and she caught their glint. Swallowing, she turned her head to the side and exposed her neck.

The proof of her trust landed in his heart and took hold.

He dipped and bit into the soft flesh where her shoulder met her neck, unable to stop himself from going deep. The second he pierced bone, his body shuddered, and he came.

Energy ripped through him, around him, even at him.

Her eyelids closed, and she gave a soft murmur.

Tension and more energy cascaded from her as her body started to heal. So, the mating had taken. He paused, his heart thundering. "Veronica?"

She breathed heavier, her body working in sleep.

He was still inside her, his mind reeling. In all his life, this was not how he imagined a mating going. He chuckled. Talk about awkward. Pressing a quick kiss to her mouth, he started to make plans. "We'll talk when you wake up."

Chapter 3

Ronni awoke suddenly and sat straight up in bed. What in the world? She looked down to see an aqua-colored teddy covering her. She fingered the soft silk, wondering how she'd ended up in it, as it had been in her bottom drawer ever since she'd won it at a bachelorette party two years ago.

Slowly, she took inventory. Her chest didn't hurt. Wow. She could breathe. Her body kind of tingled all over.

Memories assailed her. Jared and a quickie…and then nothing. Embarrassment flushed through her.

She pushed from the bed and stood, her legs easily holding her up. The mating. Feeling her neck, she found the twin bite marks. Okay.

A sound caught her attention from the other room. Now her knees weakened. She could do this. Glancing around, she saw the matching robe lying over the end of the bed. After donning it, she tied it tight, pretending it was armor. Taking several deep breaths, she moved across the room and pushed open the bedroom door. "Hello?" She moved into the living room and turned toward the kitchen.

Jared looked up from a pan holding something that smelled delicious. His thick hair was ruffled, and his chest was bare. Muscles moved in his arms and torso, while his ripped abs caught her eye. "You're alive."

Yeah. She was alive. Holy crap. How had she not taken time to appreciate his hard body? Oh, yeah. Ensuing death. She swallowed and tried to concentrate on his rugged face. "How long was I out?" she asked, her stomach rumbling.

"Four days," he said, nodding toward the small table set into the nook. "Come eat."

"Four days?" She stumbled toward the nook, remembering belatedly that she was dressed way too sexily. "Who dressed me?"

"I did." He dished up two plates of eggs loaded with veggies and some sort of meat. "I bathed you, too."

She fell into the chair. "You did what?"

He sat across from her and lifted one massively large shoulder in a casual shrug. "It became apparent that you were going to heal yourself while sleeping, so Chalton took Olivia away for a few nights. My brother was impatient with the need to mate, and since you were saved, we all figured you needed to sleep and wouldn't miss them anyway."

Ronnie took a big drink of orange juice and tried to think. So he'd bathed her. How intimate. Heat flushed into her face. "We're mated."

"Yes." He dug into his eggs, his dark gaze never leaving her face. "How are you feeling?"

Like her brains had been scrambled just like the eggs. "Stronger. Almost normal." She reached for a fork. "Am I immortal?"

"Not yet. It takes a little while for humans," he said. "But your heart sounds strong and healthy, so you're definitely on your way. If you're still feeling tingles, that's your body healing itself."

"I am." The polite conversation was eating at her.

"Then you're not all the way healed."

Yet she was going to live. Happiness bubbled up. "Um, thank you." She set down the fork to meet his gaze. She was now bound for eternity to this incredibly strong and dangerous male. Wow. "I wanted to thank you for saving my life." The man had given up a lot so she could live.

"No problem." He polished off his eggs, his gaze dropping to her neck. "The bite will never completely heal."

"Oh." She cleared her throat. "A little scar is a small price to pay for immortality."

"Isn't it though?" he murmured thoughtfully.

God, what was he thinking? She couldn't read him. Or could she? Taking a deep breath, she tried to focus on his emotions.

Strong and steel was all she got.

"What are you doing?" he asked, kicking back in the kitchen chair.

She shrugged. "Sometimes I can get feelings from people. I think I'm just intuitive."

"You're an empath. In order to mate a vampire, you must have some sort of enhancement. Psychic, telekinetic, empathic…whatever." He said the odd words as if they were everyday facts for him. "You're probably a distant cousin to the witches. That's the prevailing wisdom, anyway."

Her mouth dropped open. "No kidding." At this point, she'd believe almost anything.

"Yeah. That's probably why you became a shrink." He stood and took his dish to the kitchen. "Finish your breakfast. You need protein."

The man, or rather *male*, was sure bossy. She started eating anyway.

His phone buzzed from the back pocket of his faded jeans, and he drew it out to read the face. Those broad shoulders stiffened.

"Everything okay?" she asked, her healing heart humming.

He texted something and then turned toward her. "Are you all right here for a bit? I have some business to take care of."

"Sure." She stretched her neck. "I feel great." Actually, she could use some alone time to really try out this immortality thing. For the first time in months, she almost felt like herself. She smiled, feeling true joy.

His eyes flared with…hunger? "You're stunning when you smile, Veronica."

Her grin faltered, and different kinds of tingles exploded through her abdomen. "Thank you." She set her napkin on her plate. "We, ah, should probably set some ground rules when you get back." After she thought about what she would say.

"Agreed." From the determined set of his jaw, he thought they might argue.

Yeah. They might. "I'll finish the dishes." Craning her neck, she took stock of the disaster in her kitchen. Apparently the vampire used every pot and pan to make the eggs.

"Thanks." He strode past her and stopped, turning at the last minute.

Her chest heated.

He grasped her chin and lifted her face. "I know you're feeling stronger, but give yourself time to keep healing. You're not immortal yet, which makes you very fragile." Leaning down, he brushed his lips across hers.

Her lungs stuttered.

He released her and crossed into the bedroom, returning while still tugging a worn T-shirt over his amazing chest.

"Will I get fangs?" she asked, her mind still reeling.

He snorted. "No." By the door, he paused, turning to face her. "I'm the only one who can really bite, baby. Don't forget it." Then he left.

She stared at the closed door. Was that a threat? Should a threat make her thighs weaken and her pulse race? Wait a minute. Her pulse was actually racing. She threw back her head and laughed. For goodness' sake. She wasn't going to die.

Where was her cell phone? She stood and did a shimmy dance, finding it nicely charging on her counter. Hitting speed dial, she waited until Olivia answered.

"I'm alive!" she yelled.

"Yay!" Olivia yelled back. "I knew it. Oh, God. Can you believe it? We're immortal. We should go skydiving."

"And bungie jumping. And rock climbing," Ronni added. She paused. "Wait a minute. You're immortal, too?"

"Yep. Or I will be soon. We mated two nights ago." Olivia's voice turned dreamy. "Can you believe it? It was the most romantic night of my entire life. Chalton is beyond my dreams."

Aww. Ronni warmed, even as her heart hurt just a little. What would it be like to have love for eternity? She shook herself out of the self-pity. Damn it. She was lucky. "You deserve it, Olly. You really do."

"So do you," Olivia said. "How was it?"

Ronni snorted. "Totally awkward, to the point of panic."

Olivia chuckled. "Oh, my. That sucks. I'm sure it'll get better." She said something off the phone and then returned. "We're on a private plane and will be landing in just a few minutes. I'll grab a cab and be at our scheduled meeting in an hour. Can't wait to see you." She was silent for a beat, and then her voice lowered with emotion. "You're gonna live, Ron."

"Yeah." Ronni rubbed her chest. "I am."

Olivia yelped. "Ah, gotta go. Talk later." The phone went dead.

Ronni looked at the quiet device in her hand. What would love and mating be like? For the briefest of seconds, her stomach hurt. She shook herself out of the sadness. She was alive, and that was more than she'd hoped for just a week ago. For that, she could be immensely grateful.

And she had a job to do. Her small desk in the corner caught her eye, and she hustled for it, drawing out a stack of manila files. Each one held details about somebody who might've had the motive and opportunity to poison her. "Now, fucker. I'm going to find you."

* * * *

Jared parked his bike outside the bar, scattering slush and snow.

"You're gonna need to put the bike away for winter," his youngest brother said, leaning against the crumbling brick building outside of New York City.

"Eh." Jared shrugged off snow and followed Theo into the old Russian bar. No pool tables, dart boards, or even bright lights. Bars were for drinking, and they'd better order vodka or risk being shot by the proprietor—a thousand-year-old Russian vampire.

Theo motioned for two drinks and led the way to a scarred and scratched booth in the back. He sat. "So. You've got a mate. I can sense her on you."

Jared sat and nodded, reaching for the first shot. "Твоё здоровье!"

"Your health, too." Theo tipped back the drink.

Jared drank, letting the booze hit his stomach.

"How was it?" Theo asked, his dark eyes glimmering with amusement.

Jared grinned. "Terrible. Seriously. Just awful."

Theo winced. "Dude. Sorry about that."

The waitress brought two more shots.

"Leave the bottle," Jared said, still chuckling, his entire world settling perfectly now that his brothers were back in his life. He waited until the woman had moved out of earshot. "Veronica is beautiful and sexy, but hell. She was dancing with death. Let's just say it was a bit rushed."

Theo laughed. "That sucks, man. Have you had a chance to

redeem yourself?"

"No." Jared rubbed his whiskered jaw. "She just woke up this morning, and I figured she needed a little space. The woman looks damn good in full health, brother."

Theo's dark eyebrows rose. While his hair was a deep brown, he had the same black eyes as his older brothers. They filled with curiosity. "It sounds like you're thinking of something permanent. I mean, together type of permanent."

Jared downed his second shot of expensive vodka. "I'm not thinking anything of the sort." He'd had his one chance at love.

"Right. Good luck with that." Theo drew out a folded piece of paper. "On to business, then. I tracked down Saul Libscombe, and he has gone underground. While I wouldn't have thought he'd avenge his brother's death, who the hell knows? I'd feel better if I could find him."

Jared sighed and sat back in the booth. "Wonderful." Chalton had killed Saul's brother a few days before in self-defense. Yet another long-time family feud that just needed to be resolved, one way or another. "I don't have time for this nonsense. Both Veronica and Olivia are new mates, and they're not immortal yet. They're vulnerable."

"I know." Theo took another shot. "That's why I wanted to track down Saul."

"Where's mom?" Jared asked. "She needs shelter until we figure this out."

"She's visiting Realm Headquarters," Theo said with a grimace.

Jared stilled. The Realm was a coalition of vampire, demon, witch, and shifter nations, and it was led by Dage Kayrs, the king. Jared had always remained away from the Realm, although Chalton worked for them. "You're kidding me. She's hanging with the king?"

"Yep. Was invited and took right off. Couldn't wait to get to know the Kayrs family." Theo shrugged. "Chalton has lived with them for a century. I guess it's time we got to know his friends."

"I have enough friends," Jared growled.

Theo slapped him on the back. "Now you have more. They're good allies to have, J."

Maybe. He rubbed his eyes. "All right. Let's secure Veronica and Olivia at the safe house in Nantucket until we hunt down Saul and see his intentions."

"The house is ready," Theo said, his gaze caught by the vodka bottle. "I mean, if your mate is prepared to go underground for weeks, if not months."

Jared leaned back to study his brother. "She's my mate. She'll go where I tell her to go." While they had an arranged mating, that fact was absolute. Speaking of whom, he should check on her. He reached for his phone and stared at the screen. "Humph."

Theo looked up. "What?"

Jared bit his lip. "I don't have her number."

Theo barked out a laugh. "You don't have your own mate's phone number."

"No." Jared shook his head. "I should probably get that."

Theo started laughing too hard to reply.

The door opened, and the hair on the back of Jared's neck stood up. He slowly turned.

Theo stopped laughing. "Ah, shit," he muttered.

Jared almost stood, but the woman who'd entered quickly crossed to reach his table. "Ginny," he said, his mind nearly blanking.

She pushed a red hood off her white-blonde hair, scattering snow. "Jared. I've been looking for you." Her eyes were the clearest blue, and right now, they were scared.

"Where's your mate?" Theo nearly growled.

She shook her head. "Dead. Nearly a century ago in a witch-shifter battle. We weren't allies with the shifters then."

Dead? Her mate was dead? Jared tried to concentrate. Shifters and witches were barely allies now, even though the most current war had ended. Jared studied her. She was so small. Tiny, delicate, and obviously frightened. Where had she been? Why hadn't she contacted him before now? "Why are you here, Ginny?" he asked, his senses reeling. The woman had broken his heart two centuries ago, and he hadn't prepared for seeing her again.

"I've been on the run and this is the first time I was able to track you down." Her hand trembling, she reached out to touch his wrist. "I couldn't find you before."

Theo leaned back in the booth, irritation sizzling across his skin. "What a coincidence that you're here now. How did you find him, anyway?"

She turned toward Theo, her gaze dropping. "He just came back on the grid a few days ago. I've had feelers out for years, and this was the first chance I'd gotten to find him. Stop being mean, Theo."

Jared swallowed. Hell. This was crazy. The witch was correct in that he'd been off the grid since he'd given up being a pirate on the high seas. Theo had never liked the woman, for some reason. "Ginny, why are you scared?"

She fumbled with her wrap. "The shifter who killed my former mate is after me. He wants to finish the job."

Jared's breath caught. "Former mate?"

Her gaze lifted, so blue and deep. "I took the virus to negate the bond. I'm free, Jared. The mating bond is gone."

Chapter 4

Ronni rushed into the back room of the coffee shop, her files in a backpack and a tall latte in her hand. Her steps were sure and steady. Energized and healthy. Yeah. She was back, baby.

Two of her friends were already seated, files and papers scattered in front of them. Olivia hurried in from the bathroom, her pretty face breaking into a wide smile. "Ronni!" She rushed forward for a hug.

"You weren't kidding about making the meeting." The cabbie must've sped from the airport to the shop. Ronni hugged her best friend and leaned back to look. Olly's eyes were a sparkling blue, and she all but glowed. "You're happy."

"Yeah." Olly laughed out loud. "You will be, too. I just know it."

A man cleared his voice from the table. "What's going on? Ronni? You look tons better."

Ronni turned toward the off-duty detective. Lance Peters was about thirty with sharp green eyes, an angled jaw, and a pissed-off expression. His skin was a dark mocha, and unlike the month before, it now had a healthy glow. He'd been angry since his partner had died— supposedly of a suicide. "So do you. Is your shoulder healed?" Ronni asked.

"One little bullet won't stop me," Lance said, rubbing his shoulder after having been shot a month ago while investigating an unrelated case. "You?"

"I'm better. Maybe on the mend," she said. "Ready to figure this thing out." She turned toward Dr. Mabel Louis, the assistant medical examiner. "Any news on the poison?"

Mabel shook her head, her blue eyes clouding. "No. Nothing from your blood tests has shown the poison. It could be anything, Veronica. I won't know, I mean, until…"

"Until you can cut open my heart and take a look," Ronni said thoughtfully.

Olly slapped her on the arm. "That's not going to happen."

No, it wasn't.

Mabel flushed, her pale skin turning a bright pink. "I'm sorry to be indelicate."

"You're not. That was the plan until recently," Ronni murmured, taking a seat.

"You really do look better," Lance said, his gaze tearing across her face. "Is there a chance you'll survive this?"

"Yes," Ronni said, unable to hold back her smile.

"How?" Mabel asked, hope leaping into her eyes.

Ronni shrugged. "It's hard to say since we can't identify the poison." She cleared her throat. These were the three people she trusted most in life, which is why they were working the case off the books. The official investigation didn't seem to be going anywhere, and she had to wonder why. "Lance? Have you finished looking through yours and Walt's cases? Anything jump out?"

Walt was Lance's partner, who'd died four months previous. While his death had been ruled a suicide, the facts didn't add up. He'd been a regular psychology patient of Ronni's, as were many of the undercover cops in the precinct. His death and her poisoning had to be related, somehow.

"There are several leads in Walt's death." Lance pushed manila files across the table. "I went through your list of which cases you talked to him about, and I've cross-referenced all of them. There has to be a connection here somewhere."

Olivia took a seat and cleared her throat. "We're making an assumption that the same person who killed Walt also tried to poison you, Ronni. Walt died of an overdose."

"Walt didn't do drugs," Lance snapped.

"Yes, he did," Mabel countered softly. "We all know it. Walt was struggling after losing his wife two years ago, and we all know he drank and occasionally did drugs."

Ronni intervened before Lance could explode. "We're not knocking him, Lance. I agree, based on every session I had with him, that he wouldn't have killed himself by such an overdose." The amount shot into Walt's veins was way too much to be accidental. "Let's find out who wanted him, and then me, dead."

Lance shoved a red folder toward her. "Walt was working an internal case regarding drugs that had disappeared from lockup six months ago."

Ronni reared back. "We hadn't discussed any internal case. You think a cop took those drugs?"

Lance shrugged. "Walt did. I found the notes in the bottom of his locker at the gym."

That would make sense. A cop could easily get to her as well with the poison.

Mabel leaned forward. "You can't let anybody know you're better. They might try to take you out another way."

But she didn't know a thing about Walt's internal investigation. Did she? "I need to go through all my notes and files from meeting with Walt." She'd done so once, but her body and mind had been barely working. Who knew what she'd missed.

"I disagree," Lance said slowly, his gaze hard. "Let's get you out there and flush the bastard out."

Ronni's mouth opened and then closed. "That's a great idea. Tonight is the retirement bash for the lieutenant, right? How about I show up and prove my health?"

Mabel sputtered. "That's dangerous. You're not a cop."

Yeah, but she was flirting with immortality. "I don't care. Somebody tried to fucking kill me, and I want to know who it is. Make them pay."

"For killing Walt, too." Lance studied Mabel. "We need to take a look at your boss. He decided it was a suicide way too quickly."

Mabel paled even more. "Not necessarily. Dr. Counts has been overworked for years. He might've just missed something."

"Right. For now, I'll leave these files for you to go through. They're copies." Lance pushed away from the table. "We'll see. Tonight, everyone keep vigilant. Ronni, stick close to me. I'll cover your back."

Oh, this was crazy, but anticipation lit Ronni up.

Mabel cleared her throat. "Let's have the Tuesday meeting at the lab. I think I'm on to something with the autopsy files, and I want to have them organized for you guys to go through." She allowed Lance to assist her up and then smiled when he pressed her forward with a hand on her waist.

Were they seeing each other? "Bye," Ronni murmured, waiting until Lance and Mabel had headed back to work. "I can't wait to catch this dickhead."

Olivia sipped her latte. "What does Jared think about you pursuing the guy who tried to kill you?"

Ronni blinked. "It's not really his concern. Why?"

Olly shrugged. "I'm not sure. Chalton is over-the-top protective. I mean, he's in the other room right now doing some business while I'm just meeting with friends. I haven't given him the whole truth here."

Ronni raised an eyebrow. "Don't lie to your man for me."

"Didn't lie. Just didn't give the whole truth." Olly's eyes sparkled.

It was nice to see her friend so happy. "Don't worry about me. Jared and I have an arrangement, and he's probably already making plans to leave town." Why that made her recently healed heart ache a little, she didn't want to examine. Although it would've been fun to play with that hard body of his. She'd never seen natural muscles like that.

Olly leaned in. "Just how bad was the mating?" Her eyes widened. "Oh, no. Nobody farted, did they?"

Ronni sputtered her coffee and then laughed. "No. I didn't even have the energy to fart, and Jared was way too worried about being gentle and not breaking me."

"Well, that's good." Mirth filled Olivia's eyes. "Oh, he texted Chalton for your phone number, and I gave it to him. Figured that was all right."

"Sure." They should probably keep in touch a little.

Olivia stood. "I don't think tonight is such a good idea, you know? You're not a hundred percent yet."

"Don't care. It's time to flush this guy out." Besides, she felt fantastic. "Let's keep our investigation between us, though. Promise?" If nothing else, she needed to keep her personal and professional lives separate. Talk about having a huge secret. Vampires existed, and now she was immortal. How crazy was that?

Olivia frowned. "I'm not sure."

"Don't lie. Just don't say anything." It was too late to prove her worth to a dead man, but she could do this. Could take down an enemy.

Olivia faltered. "I don't know Jared very well, but I doubt he'd want you going after a killer on your own."

He'd done his duty, and he was gone. Ronni took another big drink of her coffee. "The vamp is probably already halfway out of town. Don't worry. I know what I'm doing."

Well, kind of.

* * * *

Jared leaned back against the door of the hotel room and crossed his arms. It had taken most of the afternoon to find a suitable place with decent security.

"Mated?" Ginny whispered, backing away. Fire flashed through her eyes. "Are you joking? You actually mated a human?" Her voice rose to shrill.

His eyebrows rose. "Yes." She was even more beautiful today than she had been centuries ago, her fragility and lady-like qualities a direct contrast to many of the women he'd met through the years. It had been a long while since they'd been in the same room. For so long, he'd imagined her perfection. Was she really that perfect?

She stared at him and then quickly dropped her gaze. In the opulent hotel suite, she looked small and a little lost. "I can't believe it." Her voice trembled.

He sighed, his mind spinning. He wanted to offer her comfort, but he couldn't touch another woman. *Wouldn't* touch another woman since he'd mated Veronica. "It was necessary."

"So you don't love her." Ginny's head snapped back up.

He opened his mouth and then shut it again. The world seemed to be closing in on him, and he needed to think it through. "I'll not discuss my mating with you." If nothing else, he owed his mate that loyalty.

Ginny paled. "I see."

Damn. He didn't want to hurt her. She was so delicate. Once upon a time, he'd wanted nothing but to stand between her and the entire world. But she'd chosen another. "You have to understand my position here," he said softly.

She nodded, tears gathering on her long lashes. "I do. This is my fault. When I let my father force me to mate Levi, I created this. I lost you."

"I would've fought your father and Levi," Jared said evenly.

"Yes, and somebody I loved would've died," she said, wringing her hands together.

Would they have? For the first time, Jared wondered. Her father had seemed like a decent guy. Would he have truly forced his only daughter to mate somebody she didn't love?

"I'm sorry, Jared," she said, a tear rolling down her face.

Of course she was. He moved forward and gathered her close, against his better judgment. How could he let her be in pain? What had he been thinking? She'd always been fragile and in need of protection.

His skin itched.

He swallowed.

His tongue swelled a little.

Clearing his throat, he backed away. The mating allergy would have him on the ground in a minute if he kept touching her. It would spread to her, too.

She looked up, another tear escaping. "The allergy."

He nodded. "Yes."

"I've no right to ask you for anything." She gestured around the suite. "I figured you'd take me to your place."

"I don't have a place in New York," he said. "You're safe here. It can't be traced to either one of us." Perhaps he could gain a secure place for her with the Realm. They were allies now, after all. "We'll figure something out."

She slowly drew her red wrap off her small body, revealing a long white dress that hugged her curves perfectly. "I need you, Jared. I always have."

"You have a family, Ginny. They can protect you, too." Had she not spent any time training as a witch? She should be able to make and throw fireballs. Had she been his, she'd know how to fight whether she liked it or not. "You need training."

"No." She sighed. "I'm not a fighter."

Veronica was. His mind moved to how hard she'd fought to stay alive to the last second, even while he had bitten her. He should call her. Hopefully she'd gone back to bed after spending the day resting.

Darkness would soon fall outside, and he wanted to check on her before the storm he smelled coming hit.

"Jared?" Ginny asked.

He shook himself back to the hotel room. "I'll find a safe place for you."

She licked her pink lips. "What about us?"

He straightened. "Huh?"

"Us." Her smile turned her pretty face into sheer beauty. "I want another chance with you. Don't you want that?"

For so long, it was all he'd wanted. But he'd given up the dream a while ago. His blood sped up. "It can't happen."

"Sure, it can. The virus works to negate a mating bond." Hope lit her eyes. "I'm proof of it."

It took a minute to catch her meaning. "Ginny." He stood straighter. "I'm mated. My mate was human and probably still is. The virus used in a mate with a still living mate might kill her." Ginny had to know him better than that. Once he'd made that commitment, it was absolute.

Ginny studied him. "Once she's strong, just think about it. If you don't love her, why stay tied for eternity? The virus really does work." She smiled. "I need you, Jared. I always have."

He had to get out of there. Too much was happening inside him...around him. And some of it was an odd guilt to be in the hotel room with another woman not his mate, regardless of the newness of his commitment to Veronica. He wasn't a guy who felt guilt, damn it. "I'll be in touch. Theo will be here to check on you soon. I texted him earlier." Seconds later, he'd shut the door.

Quick steps had him at the elevator, and soon he stood on the snowy street. Dark clouds billowed overhead like burned cotton balls and thunder rolled in the distance. What the hell was going on with the world? Ginny was free, he was mated, and all he could think about was Veronica's safety. Karma had a brutal sense of humor.

Duty called. He glanced down at his phone and quickly dialed.

"Hello," Veronica answered.

His chest settled. Her throaty voice somehow calmed his rioting emotions. "How are you feeling?"

"Fantastic," she burst out, joy in the sound. "I drank two coffees and ate a whole box of donuts. They were delicious."

He grinned. "The pictures on your mantle showed you were curvy."

"Yep." Happiness all but flowed through the line. "I like food, and it's so good to eat again. I even did a cartwheel."

Now that was something he'd pay to see. "Just take it easy. You're still healing."

"I know." She cleared her throat. "How was your day?"

He knocked his head back against the frozen bricks. "A little crazy, truth be told." While he wanted to tell her all of it, they should probably talk in person. If they were going to work together, perhaps even be friends, then honesty mattered. He owed her that.

"Oh. Do you need any help?" she asked.

He paused. She was offering to help him? When was the last time anybody had offered him help? His body warmed, head to toe. "Ah, no." He wouldn't mind talking it out, but was an ex-girlfriend something you talked about to your new mate, even if the mating was one of convenience?

"I'd like to be friends, Jared," Ronni said quietly, as if reading his thoughts.

"Me, too." He straightened up and headed for his bike. "I'll protect you. I promise."

She chuckled. "I think I'm fine. Don't worry."

She wasn't asking for anything from him. For some reason, the thought rankled. "You are not fine, not yet, and we'll discuss it when I get there." They could be friends, but he was in charge, damn it. She needed to learn that one tiny fact. He swung a leg over his bike.

"Oh. Well, I sort of have plans. How about we talk tomorrow?"

His head jerked up. "Excuse me?"

"Crap. I have to go. I'll call you tomorrow." She clicked off.

He looked down at the silent phone in his hand as if it appeared out of nowhere. What the fucking hell? Had she just blown him off and then hung up on him? He redialed her number and she didn't answer.

Fire burst through his chest. His woman needed to learn a couple of things and right now.

He pressed his brother's number with sharp stabs of his finger. Oh, Chalton's mate would know where Veronica had gone.

Then he'd have the first of many discussions with his little mate.

Chapter 5

Ronni moved in time with the beat, barely keeping from laughing out loud at the sheer exhilaration of feeling alive. The tempo was fast, which was good since she'd quickly discovered she couldn't slow dance with another man.

Her skin had flared like she'd been on fire.

Stupid mating allergy.

For now, she moved with Lance, both of them surveying the bar that was closed for the private party. Cops danced around them while many drank at round tables set throughout the place.

So far, she hadn't gotten a sense of anybody wanting to hurt her.

Her abilities were already sharper, thanks to the mating. Maybe she'd even become psychic? She'd have to ask Jared if that was possible. At this point, she'd believe anything.

The bar was dark with small red lights throughout, but the floor was clean and easy to dance on with her three-inch spiked heels. She paid special attention to Dr. Counts, the medical examiner, who drank quietly in the corner. He was around forty years old, with long blond hair and deep green eyes. Rumor had it he was dating a cop from Boston. Every once in a while, their gazes would meet and awareness would prick her. She wasn't sure with what...or if it was in her head.

Warning whispered across her arm, raising goose bumps. She turned, and Jared Reese stood in the doorway. Even across the rockin' bar filled with cops, his displeasure rode the air.

She stumbled.

Lance reached for her arm.

Jared's lips peeled back. Adrenaline flashed through her veins. "I'm okay." She moved away from Lance and toward Jared out of pure instinct. She reached him in seconds. "What are you doing here?"

He grasped her bicep, his face an implacable mask. But those eyes burned. Hot and furious, they swept her short red dress and wild hair. "I told you to stay home."

Confusion clouded her vision for the briefest of moments. "Huh?"

"Dr. Alexander?" Lieutenant Smalt moved toward her, his gait graceful, his gaze on Jared's face.

"Yes, Lieutenant?" Ronni asked, forcing a smile as her former boss moved closer. She'd always thought he was tall, but next to Jared, he seemed almost minute. And skinny. At about sixty, he had silver hair and intelligent brown eyes, and right now they took in everything about the vampire next to her.

"Is everything all right?" Smalt asked.

Her smile almost faltered. "Of course. Lieutenant Smalt, this is Jared Reese. My, ah, boyfriend." Calling Jared a boyfriend was like calling a jaguar a kitty cat.

The lieutenant held out a hand. "Nice to meet you."

Jared shook it, keeping hold of her with his other hand. "Congratulations on the retirement," he said smoothly.

So he'd spent a little time investigating her evening, now had he? She was going to kill Olivia.

"Thank you," Smalt said, looking from one to the other. "It's nice to see you feeling better, Veronica. We've been so worried." His stance was relaxed, but his gaze didn't soften.

Yeah. The man could sense a predator when one was near. Ronni leaned into Jared to defuse the situation. "I just needed rest. The illness really took a toll. I'm better now."

"I checked the status of your case, and they still haven't identified the poison," Smalt said. "Any updates I haven't seen?"

Jared stiffened to rock next to her.

"No." Ronni swallowed. They'd decided to keep the possible connection to Walt's murder quiet until they solved it. "No leads, and if I continue to get better, no autopsy on the heart."

"Well, that's good news." Smalt waved across the room at a retired group gesturing for his attention. He slapped Jared on the back.

"Nice to meet you. Take good care of our doctor here."

"I plan on it," Jared returned.

Ronni fought a shiver. When Smalt moved, she tried to edge away from Jared.

He didn't let her. "Let's talk outside." Without waiting for an answer, he drew her out the door and into the billowing snow. He glared at the storm. "Not here."

She ducked against the wind. "I'll meet you later. Right now, I have work to do." Turning, she tried to open the door. He slapped one hand against it and wrapped the other around her waist from behind. Heat flashed down her back.

"No." His hold was unbreakable.

She kicked back, nailing his shin. His inward hiss of breath made her smile. "Listen, Vamp. I have a job to do, and I don't need your help. Go do whatever you do and I'll catch up to you later." Why was her breath panting out?

"You don't need my help," he muttered, his breath brushing her hair. "All right, Veronica. Your choice. Either you come with me now and explain what the fuck is going on, or I toss your ass over my shoulder and you come with me now and explain what the fuck is going on."

Her temper stirred. "You make a move and every cop in that place will be out here."

"Every *human* cop. If I need to kick the snot out of them all, I will. Same result." The hard muscles behind her vibrated with a tension that sped up her heart.

He could probably do it, too. Damn it. His hands on her were messing with her concentration. "Fine." She pivoted right into him. "Make this quick."

"Where's your coat?" he snapped, fury darkening his high cheekbones.

She shivered, and not from the cold. "I didn't bring one." It would just get in the way.

His jaw turned to rock. "You didn't bring one." He straightened, more than towering over her. "You've been deathly ill and you didn't bring a jacket."

She rolled her eyes, trying to appear nonchalant when she kind of wanted to run screaming from his anger. No way would she let him know that, however. "I'm fine. Went from taxi to bar and planned on right back to taxi. The dress is warm."

"There's nothing warm about that dress." He jerked his leather jacket off and slapped it over her shoulders. A vein bulged in his neck, and the cords looked like they were made of raw steel.

"I'm fine." She pushed against him, the need to flee intensifying.

A second later, his nose was a whisper from hers. "Put on the coat, Veronica. God help me. Do it now." His voice sounded like he'd swallowed shards of glass with a side of raw gravel.

She slid her arms into the sleeves and tried not to tremble. "You are so bossy."

"You have no idea. Can you ride in that thing?" He glanced down at her bare legs.

Obviously he wasn't going to back down, and she sure as heck didn't want him beating up a bunch of cops. So she'd go with him and then try to get back before the party ended. She pulled the skirt up to the tops of her thighs. "Sure."

Did he just growl? She frowned into his face but couldn't read his expression.

"Good." He led her to the bike and helped her straddle it behind him. "Hold on. I'll get us there quickly."

She wrapped her arms around his firm body and leaned in, inhaling his musky scent. With the leather around her, she was surrounded by the smell and feel of raw male. Her nipples hardened beneath the dress. Damn it. She should've worn a bra.

He fired up the engine and drove quickly over very icy roads, getting them back to her apartment in record time. Okay. The guy could control a motorcycle, even in a snowstorm.

She jumped off and all but stomped up the stairs and into her apartment before whirling on him. "We need to get one thing stra—"

His mouth was on hers, his huge body driving her back into the far wall. His kiss was carnal, to the edge of being primal, hard and fast, taking more than giving. Her knees weakened, and she grasped his forearms for support.

He gave no quarter, going deeper, sliding his tongue inside her mouth. Her rapidly healing heart beat quick and wild in her chest. His mouth opened wider over hers, devouring her as if he had no intention of ever stopping. As if he had every right to plunder like the pirate he'd

He was a far cry from the man who'd so gently had sex with her the other night. "Not a chance," she gasped.

For answer, he palmed her breast.

A moan spilled out of her against her will.

"No chance, huh?" he murmured, tweaking her nipple.

She leaned her head against the wall, burning for him. "God." Giving in to what she wanted, she slid a hand inside his shirt, feeling the shocking ridges and hollows of those abs. How was he even real? Her other hand went to the hard line of his dick beneath his jeans.

He growled low. "You're playing."

"I'm not." She frantically jerked his shirt up. "Not at all." It was too good to be alive. Too good to feel like this. "More, Jared. More now."

He didn't wait for another request. One swift movement had her dress over her head and her panties snapped in two.

She fumbled with his zipper, yanking it down and freeing him. Shit, he was huge.

He grasped her butt and lifted her, impaling her with one hard push against the wall.

She cried out, pain and pleasure blending into something that burned. Her nails scored his chest, and she wrapped her legs around his waist. He started pummeling inside her, one hand across her ass, the other slapped against the wall, protecting her head and shoulders.

So easily…he held her upright.

Sparks lit her inside and she took more of him, her eyes closing. He moved her where he wanted her, his cock surging inside her, all power. The slap of flesh against flesh filled the apartment, and she could do nothing but hold on and feel.

Pure ecstasy.

She broke first, her body jerking and then exploding into miniscule pieces. To keep from screaming, she leaned in and clamped her teeth into his pec.

He growled and pounded harder, his entire body shuddering as he came.

Three more thrusts into her, almost lazy ones, and he stilled.

Her heart thundered against his chest. Little aches and pains instantly flared to life along her body. Holy crap. She leaned back against the wall, her eyelids half closed as she studied him. "So. Do we once claimed to be.

A shudder went through her entire body, branding her inside out.

He released her as suddenly as he'd kissed her, wrapping one hand around her neck.

Her pulse beat wildly against his fingers, and she could only stare at those midnight dark eyes. Hunger. Raw and untamed, hunger glinted there with a determination that stole any words she might've said.

She drew in a shaky breath. Her dress caught against her aching breasts, and she almost groaned at the painful need. Her panties wetted, dampening her thighs.

His nostrils flared, and he lowered his chin in an oddly threatening way.

Another tremble slid up her spine.

"I agree," he rumbled, his breath brushing her forehead.

She blinked. "Agree?"

"That we need to get some things straight." His hand tightened just enough to enforce his point.

Her mind finally caught back up to reality. Her back straightened with a snap. "Which would be?" It was difficult to sound defiant with his hand wrapped around her neck, but she gave it her best shot, glaring at him.

His head lifted imperceptibly. "Brave little thing, aren't you?" he mused thoughtfully.

Her knees wobbled. "You don't scare me."

His lip curved. "Liar," he whispered. "But that's not all I do to you, now is it?"

She narrowed her gaze. "Yep. That's all."

"Ah, baby." He leaned in, brushing her ear with his mouth.

Desire ripped through her, wearing claws. She bit back a moan.

"I can smell you," he whispered, his breath hot.

"Bullshit," she whispered, trying to keep some semblance of control and not rub against him for any sort of relief.

He slid a leg between hers, pressing his muscled thigh against her pounding clit. Electricity arched through her body.

Her knees gave.

"I can feel how wet you are." He chuckled, the sound low and male. "I could probably make you come like this."

She breathed out, her body primed and ready. Who was this guy?

have those things straight now?"

"Not even close." His lips twitched while his chest heaved out. "When I met you, I figured you needed saving."

"I did."

"Yes, you did. But that's not what you need now." His eyes somehow darkened even more. He kept her easily in his hold, his cock still hard enough to stay right where it was inside her.

Caution. She should feel caution, but she was too satisfied. "What do I need, Jared?"

"Why did you lie to me?" he asked, his voice a shade lower than mere curiosity.

"About what?" Desire roared inside her again, right where they remained joined. She moved a little, not surprised when he kept her in place. His strength was unreal, and the corded muscles along his arm only hinted at his power. "What did I lie about?"

"About your illness. You were poisoned." He tilted his head to the side.

Oh. That. "It's my problem, and I'll figure it out." Man, she owed him enough, considering he'd saved her life. Her father was wrong. She was smart enough to figure a good case out. For now, it would be nice if Jared started moving again.

"That's not how this works." He leaned down and nipped her lip—none too gently. "If you're in danger, I handle it. Life really is that simple, and the sooner you figure that out, the better."

She stilled. He was joking. A quick look at his face, at his hard expression, erased that thought. What year did he think it was? "Who do you think you are?"

"Your mate, baby. Apparently it's time to teach you what that means."

Chapter 6

Jared's phone buzzed before he could finish making his point. Grabbing it with one hand out of the back of his jeans, which were down around his knees, he lifted it to his ear. Not once did he release Ronni's molten gaze. "What?" he snapped.

"Meet at Grizio's Pizza for a late dinner," Chalton said without preamble. "I have news on Ronni's condition as well as Saul's case."

Jared slowly withdrew from his mate. Her eyes widened, and her body clenched as if to keep him inside. His answering grin shot color into her pretty face and irritation into her stunning eyes. "We'll be there. Call Theo."

"I already talked to Theo. He's pissed you left him with Ginny," Chalton drawled. "Please tell me you're not falling for her bullshit again."

At the moment, there was only one woman on his mind. "I'll see you at Grizio's." He clicked off.

Ronni's feet hit the floor, and she pushed him with both hands against his stomach.

He decided not to move.

Her head snapped up. "What do you want?"

Now that was a damn good question. At the moment, he wanted to bend her over the back of the sofa and fuck her hard. Very hard. But they had work to do, and he'd have to calm himself until later. "I want to figure out who tried to kill you and also ensure there are no more threats coming for us. I'm thinking we'll do that over pizza."

Interest filtered across her face. "I could eat."

"Good. We also need to get on the same page. No more hunting killers by yourself." He slid both hands down her arms.

She shoved again. "How are those abs even real?"

He looked down. "Huh?"

"Nothing. We'll talk about it later." She sidled out from the side, and he allowed it this time. "I need to grab some jeans."

"And a coat," he reminded her.

She threw him the finger and stomped into her bedroom. He grinned, his body lighting with humor. Man, taming her would be fun. He paused. Where the hell had that thought come from? Oh, he didn't mind the theme…but he hadn't planned on sticking around.

Yet, why not? Glancing down at the rumpled dress and ruined panties on the floor, his smile widened. They obviously had something in common.

Oh, yeah. He jerked up his pants, wincing as he shoved his dick back into place and zipped. Even now, the smell of her wrapped around him. Warmed him. Tempted him.

It took him several seconds to realize he'd forgotten all about Ginny.

Veronica emerged minutes later in dark jeans and a green sweater that hugged her breasts perfectly. Her thick hair was up in a ponytail, and lip-gloss covered her sweet lips.

Man, she intrigued him. She was all spunk, intelligence, and courage. It shocked him how much he liked that combination.

She took a brown leather jacket from a clothes closet. "How about we take my car?"

He shrugged and followed her outside. "So long as I drive."

"God, you're a throwback," she muttered, her sweet ass swaying down the steps.

"Yep." When they reached the car, he held out his hand for the keys.

"Fine." She threw them at his head, and he snagged them easily out of the air.

"Thanks." He slipped into the compact and put the driver's seat as far back as it would go. While she thought he was being a jerk, in truth, his reflexes were a million times faster than hers. If danger came near, he'd handle it better. Whether she liked it or not.

She huffed into the seat and secured her seatbelt.

He ignited the engine and drove out of the carport, heading even farther away from the city. "My brother has all the files about your case, and we can review them together at dinner. We've already sent a sample of your blood to our lab in Idaho, and we should have those results soon."

She dropped her chin. "How did you get my blood?"

"I texted an associate when I left the bar earlier, and he broke into the evidence locker at the station," Jared said. "Then it went on private plane and should be there today. We don't mess around."

She shook her head. "That's crazy."

"Was necessary." It would probably take some time for her to realize she was no longer human and subject to their laws. "Any clue who wanted you dead?"

"No," she said. "I think it had something to do with the death of a cop, a guy named Walt, who I saw as a patient, but I have no proof. No leads." She curled her fingers into fists on her jeans. "I also don't know how they poisoned me. I mean, many patients bring me coffee and tea, and I also drink at the station. Plus, we go out a lot as a group to a bar…"

Well, those days were over. He'd explain that to her later. For now, he had to figure this out. "Why did you become a shrink?"

"I wanted to help people." She wiped snow off her jeans. "My dad was a cop, and he said I didn't have what it took." She hunched her shoulders inward. "I guess I kind of wanted to prove him wrong. Plus, I have a knack for figuring people out."

She had a knack because she was empathic. So she was driving herself so hard just to prove herself? That wouldn't do. However, he liked that she wanted to help people. Smart, spirited, and sweet. That was her. He glanced at her, his hands easy on the steering wheel.

"What?" she asked.

"You're very likable," he said, taking a corner.

She blinked. Color tinged her cheeks. Her lips pursed. "Thank you."

Yeah. The woman knew how to take a compliment. He liked that, too. Her scent of spices and berries wrapped around him, providing comfort with a jolt of energy. The idea that somebody wanted to harm her tightened his muscles. He'd never been a nice guy, and a battle was a battle, but he'd make the asshole who'd poisoned her bleed before dying.

He pulled into the back lot of the tiny restaurant. "You ever been here?"

She craned her neck to check out the innocuous brick building. "No."

"Best pizza in the world." He jumped out of the car and crossed to assist her. "Careful. The lot is icy."

She nodded and allowed him to lead her through the back door. The smells of garlic, cheese, and pretty much heaven hit them both. She breathed in. "Wow."

"Yeah." He grinned. "You'll love it." Taking her hand, he led her through the hallways to a small private dining area and gave a nod to Theo before surveying the room. Ah, shit. Theo had brought Ginny.

* * * *

Ronni's stomach rumbled like she hadn't eaten in months, which she pretty much hadn't. If the pizza was half as good as it smelled, she'd be in heaven in about ten minutes.

Olivia rushed for her, enveloping her in a hug complete with a happy hop. "You look even better than this morning. Alive. So well." Joy filled Olly's laugh.

Ronni hugged her back, tears pricking her eyes. They were alive and would be for possibly forever. The two of them. She leaned back, smiling at the wonderful sparkles in Olly's eyes. "You look even happier."

"I am." Olly pulled her toward an empty seat. "You know Chalton and Theo." She nodded toward a stunning blonde sitting between the men across the table. "This is Ginny."

"Hi." Ronni smiled.

Ginny smiled back, but the greeting didn't meet her eyes. Was she nervous? Ronni tuned in her senses and nearly lost her breath. Tension. It was all around her. She glanced at Jared, who took the seat next to her without meeting her gaze. Interesting.

Ginny smoothed back her long hair. "Theo has been taking such good care of me." She patted his hand on the table. "I don't know what I would've done." Her voice was soft and a little timid.

"You were fine," Theo said shortly, taking a drink of what looked like beer.

"Oh, no." Ginny shook her head, her eyes widening. "We had an attack at the hotel."

Jared stiffened next to Ronni. "An attack?" He focused on Theo.

Theo rubbed a hand through his shaggy hair. "No. It was probably just a car backfiring."

The redheaded waitress entered, her notepad ready to take orders. During the hustle, Olivia leaned over to whisper. "Ginny's a witch. *The* witch from Jared's past."

Ronni stiffened. Wind whirled through her, and it took a moment for her to pin down the emotions. She was jealous? Why? She'd just met Jared. Of course, her skin held the heat from his, and her body still tingled from him taking her up against the wall. "Well, she is beautiful," Ronni whispered.

Olivia rolled her eyes. "If you like that look."

That look? Long blonde hair, bright blue eyes, flawless skin? Yeah. Who'd like that look? The woman sat directly across from them and was no doubt even more beautiful closer up.

Chalton gave them a look. Oh, yeah. Super vampire hearing. Well, who cared? Ronni and Olivia weren't changing their lives just because they'd joined up with the supernatural. "Where's her mate?" Ronni asked.

"Dead. She took some virus and came running for Jared," Olivia said, taking a sip of water from a thick plastic glass.

"Oh." A rock smashed into Ronni's stomach, heavy and painful. She reached for her own glass, and her thigh brushed Jared's hard one. Desire poured through her. One little touch and she wanted to get him naked again. But he'd done her an unbelievable favor in saving her life. If he wanted his freedom now, she had no choice but to give it to him. That had been the plan, right?

Ginny fluttered her hands together. "I just don't know what to order. What do you recommend, Jared?" From across the table, she gave a helpless shrug.

Ronni frowned. "Pizza?"

Oliva coughed next to her.

Jared nodded. "Definitely pizza." He leaned toward Ronni. "What kind do you like?"

"Loaded," she said, trying to appear nonchalant when his breath brushed her ear. Her nipples peaked beneath her sweater, and she hunched forward.

"Excellent," Jared said, his voice calm and soothing. "The fact that your appetite is back has to be a good sign."

Ginny sighed. "How nice to be able to gain weight. No matter what I eat, I stay petite."

"How sad," Olivia said sweetly.

Ronni kicked her sideways under the table. "Not me." Did Jared like the helpless and tiny type? She frowned. How irritating.

"Good. Eat up and regain those curves I saw in your pictures," he said, as if reading her mind. The waitress brought breadsticks and pitchers of beer, and he plopped two sticks on her bread plate. "I didn't ask. Do you like beer?"

"Sure," Ronnie said, nodding when he poured her a glass.

"Not me." Ginny pouted out her red lips. "Do they have wine?"

For some reason, she kept asking questions of Jared. Ronni shrugged off the desire to punch the blonde in the nose. Was he still in love with her? How the hell had he been in love with her? If that was his type, she'd give him his freedom the second she tracked down that mysterious virus.

Jared nodded. "The wine list is on the back of the menu."

Ginny's eyelashes fluttered. She made some sort of odd noise. "What do you recommend, Jared?"

Theo took her attention and drew a menu up to her face.

Oliva leaned close to whisper, "Did she just simper? I've never seen a simper before. I think that was a fucking simper."

Ronni bit her lip, trying not to laugh.

Jared turned and patted her on the back, nearly knocking her into the table. "You okay?"

"Yes," she gasped, reaching for her water.

He eyed her, his gaze dark. "You sure? Maybe you should still be resting for a while. It might take time to get better. Perhaps this was a bad idea." He moved to stand.

She grabbed his hard thigh and pressed down. "I'm fine. Really. Starving."

He glanced down at her hand, and hunger flared in his eyes. Not for pizza. He looked like he could eat her whole, and right then and there.

She swallowed and started to move way. His palm flattened over hers, he sat back down, and he held her in place. Heat from his thigh warmed her palm, and then he clenched his muscle.

Her breath caught.

Her jeans became too tight. As if the dinner wasn't uncomfortable enough, now her skin was sensitized and needy. "This is all just too weird," she muttered.

"Tell me about it," Jared said from the corner of his mouth.

She coughed out another laugh.

"Eat," Jared said, pushing her bread plate toward her. "I want you healthy."

Why? So he could push her up against the wall again? Or so he could get a virus and then go on to mate the pale beauty staring at them? That twit couldn't make him happy. Ronni bit into the breadstick, and the taste made her hum in pleasure.

Jared cleared his throat. "What do we know, Theo?"

Theo kicked back in his chair, his shaggy hair around his collar. "Saul Libscombe has popped back into circulation. He's in South Africa running a refuge right now."

"Is he a threat?" Chalton asked, sliding his arm over Olivia's shoulder. "I did kill his brother the other day."

"In self-defense," Theo murmured.

Chalton nodded. "Yeah, but do you think he'll come after us?"

"Not at the moment," Theo said. "He could be preparing for an attack, but it doesn't look like it to me."

"He's always been a decent guy," Jared said thoughtfully. "Let's keep eyes on him."

"Done," Theo said, reaching for his beer.

"What about the poison in Ronni's blood?" Jared asked.

Theo shook his head. "Our labs haven't identified it yet, but they will. The more interesting question is how was she poisoned?"

"I don't know," Ronni said. "Could be a number of ways." She'd gone over it so many times in her mind, and no answer came clear.

"It had to be somebody close to you," Chalton said quietly.

"Not necessarily," she said. "I've thought about it. Anybody could've spiked a drink at the club or even at work. And some poisons are deadly enough that one dose is all it takes to attack a heart."

Jared nodded. "True. We'll get you underground until we figure it out."

Ronni reared up. "Not a chance in hell." As her temper stirred, she caught a small smile crossing Ginny's face from across the table.

Jared leaned in. "We'll discuss it later, Mate."

Chapter 7

Jared ignored the daggers shooting from Theo's eyes as they escorted the women into the parking lot. He had his hands full with getting Veronica healthy, and Theo could just cover Ginny until she headed home to her family. She was smart and obedient and easy to protect.

Which was the exact opposite of Veronica. Oh, she was intelligent, but she truly didn't realize how fragile she was. It was his job to teach her that, no matter how much he admired her spunk.

Ginny cast him a longing glance, and he tried to give her a reassuring smile.

At the moment, he had to focus. He'd made a commitment to Veronica, and he wasn't the type of guy to put his mate in danger, convenience or not.

Plus, he wasn't the youthful man he'd been centuries ago when he'd fallen for Ginny. Odd that he hadn't realized that fact until meeting Veronica. His emotions jumbled, and he cut through them with hard logic. Veronica was his responsibility, period. A niggling voice in the back of his head laughed at him. At his cold logic.

Wind whipped around them, and he pivoted to shield her the best he could. Lovely color had filled her face after eating the delicious pizza, and her movements were smooth and graceful instead of the cautious and shaky she'd shown before the mating.

She was on the mend.

Every once in a while, out of the blue, it hit him how close the world had come to losing her forever. To having her light and energy disappear. He growled.

She glanced up, snow on her long eyelashes. "You okay?"

"Fine." He scouted the quiet street alongside the parking lot. Whoever had poisoned her would beg for a quick death.

The air changed just enough to give him pause. His body tightened instinctively. "Chalton—" he started, just as his brother pivoted toward the street.

Tires screeched. A car careened into view, the weak moonlight glinting off the barrel of an assault rifle. Pattering instantly filled the night. Jared leaped toward Veronica, flattening her on the ice and covering her with his body.

Her breath whooshed against his throat.

The car slid to a stop, and the driver half leaned out the window, taking aim. A mask covered his face.

Shit. Jared rolled Veronica around the nearest SUV, taking cover. Ice slid down his shirt. "Status?" he bellowed.

"Not hit," Theo snapped from behind a blue truck.

"Help, Jared," Ginny cried out, her voice high and frightened.

"She's covered," Theo yelled before Jared could reply.

Veronica shoved against him, and he crouched to his knees. Bullets pinged off metal, and he ducked his head, keeping her between him and the car taking the assault. "Chalton?"

"We ducked back inside," Chalton returned, slowly opening the back door, hunching low.

Good. Olivia must be secured inside.

A bullet ripped into Chalton's shoulder, and he dropped, blood bursting from his shoulder. "That asshole dies tonight."

Jared leaped for his brother and yanked him down behind the car. "How bad?"

"Bad enough to piss me off." Chalton clamped a hand over the wound, fury sizzling along his hard face. "We're pinned down."

"There might be more coming," Jared muttered, ducking again when more bullets pinged over his head. "I think a full frontal assault would be best. You stay here and cover Veronica."

She grabbed his arm, her eyes widening. "What in the world? You're not rushing a guy with a gun."

But he wanted the fucker's neck in his hands. Jared sighed. "Fine." He grabbed a gun from his boot. "Then I'll just shoot him."

"Good plan," Veronica sputtered, reaching down and removing a small caliber pistol from along her calf.

Jared's mouth dropped open. "You're packing?" he growled.

She rolled her eyes. "Somebody wants me dead. Of course I'm packing."

He couldn't help it. In the middle of a firefight, in the midst of a temper, he smiled. God, she was perfect. "Just keep your currently human head down, woman. A bullet could still kill you."

"Understood," she said, angling toward the front of the vehicle to aim her weapon.

She apparently didn't understand shit. His grin widened, even as he jerked her back with his fingers curled into her waistband.

She slid toward him on her knees, her back to him, unable to fight him on the ice. "What are you doing?"

"Keeping you safe." He pressed a hard kiss to the back of her head. "Let me."

Did she just growl?

Another car slid into sight.

"Second gunman," Chalton muttered, tugging a gun out from beneath his jacket.

Jared angled up and fired several times over the hood. The first driver ducked back behind his door, while the other slid out the far side of his vehicle to shoot over his own hood.

"Livy, stay down," Chalton yelled as the back door of the building started to open.

It instantly closed.

Bullets came from Theo's direction, as did a woman's high-pitched scream.

"It's okay, Ginny," Jared hissed. The woman needed to stay quiet, damn it. She'd just given Theo's location away.

"Can't she throw fire or something?" Veronica muttered, crouching as more bullets cascaded above their heads.

All witches threw fire. It was too bad Ginny didn't know how to fight. "Right now, she just needs to stop screaming so we can get rid of these guys. I need one of them alive," he said.

Chalton nodded. "Affirmative." He reared up and fired a volley of shots toward the attackers.

A human male screamed in pain.

Good enough. Jared launched himself over the hood of the car, zigzagging on the ice and firing toward the closest car.

The other car zoomed off with the smell of blood in its wake.

Bullets whizzed by his head, and he increased his speed. The rancid smell of fear hit him right before the asshole shooting at him dove into his car and slammed the accelerator down. The car fishtailed, zooming down the icy street.

Jared turned to make sure everyone was all right. Bullet holes lined the brick building behind them.

A quick survey showed everyone getting to their feet, nobody bleeding.

Fury swept through him to turn colder than the ice beneath his feet. "Stay here." Turning, he barreled into the street, turning and launching into a run after the speeding car. It was icy, and the driver was sliding up ahead.

Oh, fucker. You're gonna die.

* * * *

Ronni gasped as Jared dodged bullets and the gunman drove off. Her hands shook, and her body ached from being pummeled to the ground. She took a deep breath. Okay. They were all safe.

Then Jared lowered his chin and ran full bore after the fleeing vehicle.

"Jared," she yelled, shoving around the damaged car and running after him.

"Ronni, wait—" Chalton reached to grab her, his fingers scraping along her arm.

She lifted her gun and ran after Jared, her feet sliding on the ice. Her boots skidded across the asphalt, and her arms windmilled to regain her balance. She turned, her breath panting white into the freezing air.

Several yards ahead, Jared reached the Buick and grabbed the trunk, using the leverage to flip himself up on the roof.

What the holy hell was he doing? "Jared, damn it!" Careful not to fall, she tried to find traction along the side of the road to keep moving forward. A sound behind her caught her attention, and she partially turned to see Chalton on her heels, blood flowing from his chest.

"He's crazy," Ronni bellowed, turning again for the road.

Jared crouched on the roof of the speeding vehicle, his body stiffening as he lifted his arm back to apparently punch through the metal.

The driver hit the brakes.

Ronni yelled again as the car turned into a wild spin. Jared grabbed the windshield wipers, and his legs flew out from the car. The vehicle crashed into an abandoned brick building, throwing him across the road.

He bounced three times, leaving huge divots in the ice and asphalt.

"Jared," she breathed, reaching him and sliding on her knees. "Oh, God. Are you okay?" She leaned in and grabbed his face. "Jared?"

He clasped her hands and stretched to his feet, giving her no choice but to follow. Blood flowed from a cut above his left eye, and his cheekbone was turning purple. "I told you to stay put." Pushing her behind him, he advanced on the now silent car.

A gun appeared through the driver's window.

"Fuck." He jumped forward, kicking the gun back into the car.

A man howled in pain from within.

Growling like an animal, Jared ripped off the door and sent it spinning through the air. It fractured in the center of the street and slid several yards back toward the restaurant.

Holy crap, he was incredible. Her stomach warmed, even as she kept her distance. How out of control was he?

He manacled the man inside by the neck and lifted him from the car, smashing him back into the metal several times. Metal crunched, and the guy cried out in pain.

Finally, Jared stopped beating on him, and the guy hung limply, his body heaving.

Jared ripped off his face mask. "Who is he?" Jared growled.

Ronni inched forward as Chalton took position next to her. The guy had blond hair, a series of tattoos down his neck, and cloudy brown eyes. "I don't know," she said softly, looking him up and down.

"Who were you shooting at?" Jared asked, his face an inch from the blond's.

The blond swallowed, and a snot bubble dropped from his nose. "It was just a job," he stuttered.

"Who?" Jared asked, smacking him back against the car again.

The guy wheezed. "Please let me go."

"Talk before I break your neck," Jared snarled.

Next to the injured man, Jared looked like the pirate he'd once been. Deadly, pissed, and lacking in mercy.

Tears filled the guy's eyes. "Her. I was hired to shoot her." He jerked his bleeding head toward Ronni.

She winced. That was going to get the guy hurt, without question. "Who hired you?" she asked, keeping her distance. His eyes pleaded with her for help, and she steeled herself. He'd tried to kill her.

He shook his head. "I don't know. Marcel asked for my help. He got away."

"Marcel who?" Jared asked, shaking the guy.

"Johnson. One-twenty-five Newark Street," the man said, almost eagerly. "He was a buddy of a cellmate I had in prison. We met up last week, and he hired me for the job—but I have no idea who hired him. That's all I know. Honest."

"Okay." Jared snapped his neck.

Bile rose in Ronni's throat, and she swallowed it ruthlessly down. Her vision went black. Oh, God. Jared had just killed the guy without a second thought. As she tried to regain her balance, she watched him shove the body back into the car.

Dizziness attacked her, and her ears turned hot. Blood rushed through her veins. Her eyes rolled back in her head, and her body fell. The last thing she heard was Jared yelling her name.

Chapter 8

Jared finished going through the immaculate and organized files in Veronica's desk. She'd done a thorough job of working her own case, complete with a massive suspect list.

Yet one by one, she'd crossed them off.

She was too sweet to see that somebody had wanted her dead. He looked over to study her sleeping on the sofa. The woman breathed easily, and more tingles cascaded from her as her body continued repairing itself.

When she'd fainted, he'd nearly lost his mind. What had he been thinking, allowing her out of the apartment and into danger when she was still healing? As a mate, so far he sucked.

Being a pirate had been so easy. He'd taken over a ship, pillaged it, and sent its occupants home. If there had been women, he'd invited them to stay, but if they wanted to go home, he'd secured them safe passage. While often they wanted to return home, he'd had more than a couple stay with him for a while.

Oh, he'd always compared them to Ginny's gentle beauty, and they'd always been temporary.

Yet when he compared Veronica to Ginny, his blood surged. Veronica was spirit and defiance, and she brought something out in him that felt energized. Absolute. Primitive.

As a young man, barely more than a boy, he'd loved how strong Ginny made him feel. How needed.

Yet now he admired Veronica's strength, even if she didn't realize how fragile she could be. His feelings were darker...more powerful now. What the hell did that all mean?

More importantly, how was he going to keep a mate safe who didn't want to be kept safe?

Breaking her wasn't an option, and taming her would take centuries.

Unless she tamed him. He grinned.

She blinked awake. "Your grin gives me pause," she whispered, pushing hair off her forehead.

"So you do have an ounce of self-preservation," he returned, his heart warming that she'd awakened.

She rolled her eyes and sat up. "You broke that guy's neck."

"Yes, I did," he said evenly. "If there's a threat to you, they die." There weren't any softer words to use, so he didn't bother searching for any. "Realize and accept that now, because it's not going to change."

"I don't need you fighting my battles." A slight bruise covered her chin from when he'd tackled her to the ground.

"That's unfortunate." He leaned forward, making sure he had her absolute concentration. "I understand your need to prove yourself, even though your father is dead. I get it. And I even sympathize with it. However—" He held up a hand as she started to protest. "I'm not on board with you putting yourself in danger because of that need. Get over it, take care of it, and knock it off."

"Or what?" she snarled, her lip twisting.

He blinked. His chest heated, spiraling out. "Oh, baby. You are not strong enough yet to challenge me." Putting warning into his tone, he kept her gaze until she blinked. "I enjoy your spunk, but stop pushing."

"Oh, because you like simpering, weak women, right?" She rolled her eyes. "Whatever. I can't believe you like a woman who hides who she really is. What is wrong with you? Do you honestly need an ego stroke that badly?"

Whoa. That was quite a mouthful. "I guess we'll talk about this right now, then." He set the files to the side. "I was in love with Ginny lifetimes ago when I was much younger. My commitment is to you, and I have no intention of changing that. Ever."

Veronica snorted.

His temper stretched awake.

Her pretty eyes flashed fire. "You can use the word commitment all you want, but buddy…you don't want that woman. Not even a little bit."

Did she just call him *buddy*? It was a slight, and she'd meant it as such. "Watch yourself, Veronica."

"Why?" Her chin jutted out. "Are you getting pissed I'm insulting your one true love? The bitch that actually mated somebody else when you would've killed for her?"

His head reared back. Jealous? Veronica was jealous. He couldn't prevent his lip from twitching as he settled down. "Calm yourself, and do it now." Her face was getting red, and the healing tingles had stopped. Her heart required more healing, and she needed to concentrate to do that. Everything else could wait.

The red bloomed into fury. Her fingers curled into a fist. "You are such a prick."

All right. Name calling would not do. "I'm trying real hard here to hold on to my temper, darlin'. While I know you won't simper, I strongly recommend you simmer down and now."

She snarled. "Or what, dickhead?"

He breathed out, his breath on fire. "Or you struggle sitting for the next fucking week."

She reared back. "Oh, you—"

"Stop," he snapped. "I'm not fucking with you. One more insult, one more name, and I will fucking turn you over my fucking knee." He didn't want to. He wanted to talk rationally with her. Yet her temper prodded his, especially when he hadn't done anything to deserve it. The woman couldn't hold him responsible for feelings he'd had as a kid centuries before she was even born.

For once, she seemed to heed his warning. Her eyes darkened, and her gaze ran over him. "You're still bloody and dirty."

"Yes. I wanted to make sure you awakened before taking a shower." It was nearly midnight, and he needed some rest. He stretched his neck, his body humming. Getting away from her for a few moments held certain appeal. Unless…"Would you like to join me?"

She studied him, confusion and anger still blanketing her features. "No."

Fair enough. If she needed time to process him, to come to grips with his way of dealing with threats, he could grant her that. "All right. There's tea on the stovetop. Have some to warm yourself up." Without waiting for an answer, he stood and headed for the bathroom.

A rap on the door stopped him short. He pivoted and headed to open it, wanting to sigh at seeing Theo and Ginny in the hallway. "What is going on now?" He moved aside to allow them in. It was way too late in the evening for visitors.

Theo rubbed dirt off his jaw. "An attack squad moved in at the hotel, and we were warned just in time to get out. Satellite feeds monitored by the Realm."

Jared checked the hallway and shut the door. "Attack squad?"

Theo slid his gun to his waist. "I had soldiers move in as we got out and don't have a report yet. As soon as they check in, I'll let you know."

Jared sighed. "All right. We're leaving here in an hour. We have another safe house we can use."

"I'm not leaving," Veronica piped up, her gaze on Ginny.

At that moment, he'd just had more than enough. He turned on his mate. "You are leaving. I'm giving you one hour to pack what you'll need for at least a week, until I find the guy who tried to poison you and break his neck." His voice went hard and low as he let his temper loose. "If you don't pack, you'll go in the clothes you have on."

She stood, fury in her eyes, apparently oblivious to the newcomers. "You wouldn't dare."

"I would." He was done with all of them. "Theo? Handle things here for fucking ten minutes. I need a shower." Stomping across the apartment, he slammed the bedroom door.

Jesus. He needed to calm down.

* * * *

Ronni barely kept from flinching as the door banged. She glared at Theo. "If your brother made any of my paintings drop, he's paying for them."

Theo snorted. "So the mating is going well, is it?" He scratched his head. "I have some things in the car and will be right back." His gaze went from Ginny to Ronni. "Ah, don't kill each other." Whistling, he let himself out and into the darkness just as his cell phone rang.

Ginny fluttered her hands together. "I'm so sorry to intrude at such an inappropriate late hour."

Ronni rolled her eyes, her entire body exhausted. It was way past her bedtime. "The big strong men are gone. Give it a rest, would you?" She turned and loped into the kitchen. "Would you like some tea?"

Ginny stared at her, calculation in those blue eyes. "I really would. You know you can't hold on to Jared, right? He's been in love with me for centuries."

Ronni winced. Well, she'd wanted Ginny to drop the act. "It seems to me that a guy like that wouldn't forgive a betrayal, you know?" She poured two cups of steaming tea. "His love for you probably ended a long time ago."

"Neither one of us believes that," Ginny said smugly, looking around the small apartment.

Ronni added sugar cubes to the tea. "I have to ask. When we were attacked, did you even think of throwing fireballs?" How cool would that talent be? She'd love to see it actually happen.

"No." Ginny drew off her red cape. "I allowed Theo to shield me, of course."

What a waste of a good ability. "You really think that's what a guy wants?" She crossed around the counter and carried the tea toward Ginny, who sat on the sofa.

"Yes." Ginny accepted the tea, smoothing down her long skirt.

"Not a guy I'd want," Ronni said thoughtfully, taking a sip.

"Which is why you and Jared simply don't mix," Ginny said. "Sorry."

Ronni perched on the adjoining chair. "Eh. I'm not sure about that. Lady, you really need to enter the current century. It's okay to be strong."

Ginny fluttered her eyelashes. "We all have our places. Mine is with Jared. Finally." She took a sip of her tea, somehow doing it daintily. "You're not going to win, so how about you just get out of my way?"

Ronni rubbed her nose. "You know, I like Jared." Even though sometimes he acted like an asshat from the last century, he seemed like a decent guy. He had saved her life, after all. Plus, he was a god in bed, and they'd only really had one good marathon. "I think I'll do him a favor and keep him away from you." It was the least she could do.

Ginny sniffed. "I like your confidence, but it isn't going to happen."

Ronni forced a smile. How in the world had Jared fallen for this woman? Was he really that simple? The hot sense of possessiveness sweeping through her nearly stole her breath. "Wanna bet?" she murmured.

Ginny's eyes flared. "You're messing with a witch. Perhaps you should remember that fact."

Ronni's back straightened. "Why? What are you going to do? Whine me to death?"

Ginny set her tea down with a sharp snap. "I'm warning you."

Anticipation lit Ronni from within, and she slid her teacup onto the nearest table. "Are you? How so? Gonna start crying?" Something in her just couldn't stop goading the blonde.

"No." Ginny reached out, almost casually, and slapped Ronni across the face.

The sound echoed throughout the living room. Pain dug through Ronni's skull. Fury lanced through her on the heels of astonishment. "Oh, yeah?" Bunching her knees, she leaped over the coffee table and tackled Ginny into the sofa.

Ginny shrieked and shot her fingers into Ronni's hair, pulling hard.

Pain careened along her scalp, and tears pricked Ronni's eyes. "Don't pull hair," she muttered, jerking free and straddling the blonde. "Hit like a woman." She punched Ginny in the face, her swing slightly off.

Ginny screamed and dug her nails into Ronni's neck, shoving her onto the coffee table and following to land on top of her. Cups and a couple of books scattered. Ronni struggled, and Ginny reared back and punched her in the mouth.

Pain exploded along Ronni's mouth. "Thatagirl!" She levered back and punched Ginny in the neck, throwing the woman off her and onto the floor.

Ronni rolled off the table, already swinging, the taste of blood in her mouth.

Ginny kicked up, nailing her in the chin. Her head snapped back, and she fell against the chair, making it skid several feet toward the kitchen. Holy hell. The woman had a good kick. "Now we're talkin',"

Ronni said, standing and wiping blood off her lip.

"You are such a bitch." Ginny shoved to her feet.

"Eh," Ronni said. "Jared likes that about me."

Ginny shrieked and rushed her, tackling her toward the kitchen. Ronni struggled, throwing blows and trying to avoid those sharp nails.

"What the fuck?" Jared rushed in from the bedroom wearing just his jeans, which he hadn't had time to button. His wet hair curled around his neck and was slicked back from his hard face. He reached them just as Theo burst through the front door.

Jared grabbed Ronni by the armpits, while Theo grasped Ginny. Ronni shoved an elbow back into Jared's gut, aiming a punch at the other woman's throat. Her fist glanced off, and Ginny kicked her in the knee.

"Knock it off." Jared twisted, pulling Ronni to the side and manacling her from behind. She struggled against him, but he trapped her arms at her sides.

Theo had a hold of Ginny, who kicked against him, fighting to get back at Ronni.

"Stop it!" Jared roared.

Both women stilled.

"What the hell are you two doing?" he bellowed, giving Ronni a slight shake.

Ginny stopped fighting. Her breath heaved out of her, and her hair was a wild mess of blonde.

Ronni smiled. "You're becoming likable finally."

Ginny snorted, amusement filling her eyes. Then quickly, she sobered, and a veil dropped.

Ronni paused. Whoa. Wait a minute. Her gaze narrowed.

Ginny blinked, and her bottom lip trembled. "She attacked me."

Ronni peered closer. What was the woman doing? Hiding? Who was she?

Jared's hold didn't lessen. "Theo? I think you should take Ginny to the safe house now. My mate and I will be along in a little while. Apparently we need to have a discussion first."

Oh, he was not taking the blonde's side. He just was not. Ronni stomped his foot.

His hold tightened, and he lifted her several inches off the floor with just an arm banded around her waist.

She dangled like a total dork. "Put me down." She kicked back again.

His arm flexed, cutting off her air. "Settle," he murmured.

She went limp against him, not having much of a choice. His hold relaxed enough she could breathe again. Oh, she wanted to call him a total dick, but she wasn't quite that brave. His threat from earlier still rang in her ears.

Ginny shrugged Theo off. "She's not right for you, Jared."

Jared sighed, his chest moving Ronni's body. "We are not dealing with this right now. Theo? What is going on?"

Theo kept a good hold on Ginny. "You know what is going on. I came in and they were rolling around like we used to as kids."

"That's not what I meant, damn it. Have our soldiers checked in from the hotel?" Jared snarled.

"Yes. It turns out there is somebody after sweet Ginny here." Theo frowned. "Our guys took on a squad of shifters. Good fight, but they didn't get a chance to take a prisoner before the human cops turned up."

"Damn it," Jared muttered.

Ronni gasped. "Did you say shifters? As in actual shifters? People who changed into animals like on television shows?"

Ginny grinned and then quickly sobered. "For goodness' sake." She smoothed down her rumbled blouse. "Shifters are just another species on earth. A powerful species." She frowned. "They can hunt or track anybody."

Did she just smile for a second? Ronni studied the witch. Something was definitely off, but she couldn't figure out what.

"The shifters are after you because of your mate?" Jared asked, his breath brushing Ronni's hair.

"Put me down," Ronni muttered.

"Quiet." Jared emphasized the order with a hard shake. "Ginny?"

The blonde nodded. "Yes. It's a long and sordid tale of families at war. You know. Typical of our people. I think I can handle it."

Wow. Look who was all independent all of a sudden. Ronni cleared her throat, feeling like a rag doll suspended in the air.

Jared ignored her. "I can't let you take on a shifter by yourself."

Theo grasped the blonde's arm. "I've got this. Take it as a mating gift."

Ginny jerked free. "I don't need your assistance, Reese junior."

"Too fuckin' bad," Theo snapped. "Let's go to the safe house, and we'll figure it out."

Ronni swallowed.

Ginny stopped struggling. "I'm finally trying to leave you, and now you want to get involved. Release me. Now."

Sincere. For the first time, the woman sounded sincere. Ronnie tried to read her, to get an emotion, but everything was just too jumbled.

Theo growled. "The shifters are now after me, so we're hitting the safe house and you're going to tell me everything." Anger buzzed along his voice, and he looked every inch the dangerous vampire.

"What a kind offer." Ginny smiled, transforming her face into sheer beauty, even with the sarcasm. "Jared? Tell your brother to back off, please."

Jared was silent for a moment. "We'll meet you at the safe house, Theo. In about an hour."

Ginny frowned. Theo took her arm and opened the door. Seconds later, they were gone.

Jared lowered Ronni and flipped her around, planting her on her feet. His eyes glinted a deadly black, and even barely dressed, danger oozed from him. "What the hell were you thinking?"

Chapter 9

Ronni's mouth dropped open, and pain sliced through her heart. The man was mad at her because she'd fought with his precious Ginny? "Screw you, Jared." She tried to shove away from him, but he manacled her biceps and held her in place. Easily.

He gave her a slight shake. "Your heart is still mending." He bit out each word with a low growl.

She frowned. "Huh?"

He gave her a slight shake, as if he couldn't help himself. "You're not healed yet, and you just got in a fistfight with a four-hundred-year-old witch. Where in the hell is your damn brain?"

She blinked. "You're worried about *me*?"

He looked at her like she'd completely gone insane. "Yes. One of us has to worry about you. You're crazy. Nuttier than a fucking fruitcake. You've got bats in the belfry. You're off the wall. Around the bend." He sucked in air. "Or in the vernacular of the day, you're fucking cray cray."

She couldn't think. Had a four-hundred-year-old vampire just called her *cray cray*? "You've lost your mind," she stuttered.

"Yes. Yes, I have," he said, his eyes wild. "One week of being mated to you and I've lost any semblance of sanity I ever had. Listen here, woman. I'm wild. I'm the crazy one. You will not turn me in to the voice of reason. I won't allow it."

She breathed out. The man was completely losing it. "Maybe you should sit down."

He looked at the disaster in the living room and then back to her.

Reaching out, he gently wiped blood off her lip. "You were fighting over me." Amusement finally darkened his tone and brought him back to reality.

"Were not," she snapped, her lip tingling.

"Were too." He leaned in and licked her mouth.

Sparks zipped through her, lighting every nerve on fire. "I was not," she murmured against his mouth.

"Pretty girls who lie get punished." He kissed her, being gentle, making her forget all about being punched in the face. "Would you like to be punished?"

Her body did a full-on tremble that ended with her pressing her thighs together as her clit ached. She kissed him back, sliding both hands up and over the hard ridges of his bare chest. "You have got to stop threatening me," she murmured, digging her nails into his firm skin.

He kissed along her jawline and nipped her earlobe. "Isn't a threat if I fully plan on carrying through. Is more like a promise, don't you think?"

She chuckled and angled her neck so he could have better access. They had so much to figure out, and yet she wanted to keep on touching him. Keep on being touched by him. "These feelings. Are they because of the mating?" There had to be a rational explanation.

"No. They're because I've lost my mind and I doubt you ever had yours." He tunneled his hands through her hair and leaned in to kiss her, still gentle but somehow insistent.

Why did she get the feeling he always held back? "Stop treating me like I'm fragile."

"You are fragile." He slid his tongue into her mouth. "You'll always be fragile."

She paused. "I won't get stronger?"

"No. You'll become immortal with no extra strength or powers." He leaned back, a frown drawing down his eyebrows. "Didn't I explain that?"

"Nope." Shoot. She was planning on becoming a serious immortal badass. Oh, well. She could punch with the best of them right now, and she was a damn good shot with a gun. "So no extra abilities?"

He ran his thumb down her cheekbone, spreading warmth along her skin. "Your empathic abilities will increase, and you'll gain my ability of abnormally fast reflexes, probably. But no extra strength."

Well, it would be cool to be super-fast. That was something. At some point, he had to see her for her strengths. "I could've taken Ginny, you know."

Displeasure curved his mouth. "It's silly for you two to fight. Don't let it happen again."

She reared back. So much for arousal. "You have got to stop telling me what to do." She'd ask if he still loved the blonde, but did it matter? They were temporary, and he had a right to his life again. After she'd regained all her strength. Stepping away from him, she tried to calm her raging hormones. "Enough is enough, Jared."

"You're my mate," he said, his chin lowering.

"So the hell what?" She put both hands on her hips. "Aren't you leaving town soon?"

"No." A gleam she couldn't recognize glinted in his eyes. "I'm staying right here to keep you alive and out of trouble. Turns out it's going to be a full-time gig."

Oh, he did not. "Thanks, but no way." She reached down and started replacing the books onto the coffee table.

"Did you pack?" he asked.

She rolled her eyes. "I was a little busy throwing punches with your ex-lover."

"Never slept with her." He glanced at his wristwatch. "You have fifteen minutes to gather whatever you need. We're leaving here."

They'd never slept together? Was that why he'd never gotten over the woman? It was the curiosity? The wondering? The one who got away? "Why do we have to leave?" she snapped.

"Because apparently whomever is after you has hired hit men. Remember the guys shooting at us after our nice pizza dinner? I'm thinking staying at your apartment isn't the wisest course of action."

Well, when he put it like that. Even being sarcastic, the vampire was somehow sexy, yet she needed to concentrate. "My attending the retirement party did flush out somebody. What do they think I know?" Whatever it was, Walt hadn't shared. Why wouldn't they believe that? If she knew anything, she would've come forward by now.

Jared shook his head. "I don't know, but I have a team investigating."

She caught herself. "A team?"

"Yes. Forensic and detail team. They're going through all e-mails from the station, tracing your movements and Walt's. They'll find out what happened." Jared moved toward the kitchen. "Go pack, Veronica."

A team? "They won't go through my patient files, right?" What kind of team could a vampire put together anyway?

Jared shrugged. "Probably." He held up a hand when she started to lambast him. "They don't care about your patients and won't let any information leak. But they will be thorough."

"Who are these people?" she asked.

"Computer experts as well as private detectives. Some vampires, some shifters, and probably a witch or two. They're the best." Jared put a dish in the dishwasher. "We're leaving in ten minutes, packed or not."

She gave him a look and hustled toward the bedroom. What exactly did one wear to a safe house?

Her phone buzzed, and she quickly read a group text message from Mabel. "Don't forget we're meeting at the lab tomorrow. I'm on to something."

Good. Finally. "We're taking my car," she called out to Jared, tossing jeans into a bag. Then she added a couple of sweaters, some boots, a pocketknife, and her small gun. It was time to figure this thing out.

* * * *

Jared finished scoping out the safe house. Three stories made up the opulent house set on three acres far outside of the city. "This place is nice," he whistled, making sure the windows on the ground floor were locked. Snow pelted against the darkened windows as the night pressed in around them.

"Uncle Benny owns it," Chalton whispered. "Mom talked him in to letting us stay here."

Jared winced. "Does he still want you dead?" Maybe staying there wasn't such a great idea.

"Not sure," Chalton said. "It wasn't really my fault his penthouse got bombed, you know." He rubbed his chin and leaned against the doorframe. "Okay. It was my fault. But I paid for the repairs and signed over my house in Barcelona for him as an apology."

Yeah, but Benny was crazy. "Well, on the bright side, Benny is in Russia still. He won't try to kill you until he's back in the States."

Chalton nodded, his gaze serious. "Yeah. That's my analysis, too." A grin slowly spread across his face. "Uh, Theo said Ronni and Ginny got in a fistfight over you?"

Jared sent him a look. "Theo's a gossipy old woman."

Chalton laughed and headed for the stairs. "I like that about him. Have a nice night."

Jared followed suit, walking down a long hallway to a sprawling bedroom at the end. Veronica was already in bed, her back turned to the door. He engaged the lock and shrugged out of his clothes, leaving a gun on the bedside table.

Sleet slapped into the windows as the storm increased outside.

He lifted the covers and slid inside, pulling Veronica into his body. She was all softness and curves, sweetly relaxed in near slumber. Her smell of spices and woman surrounded him, and he breathed her in. His entire life, he'd remember her scent.

"Are you all right?" she asked sleepily. "Being thrown from that car had to hurt. I should've asked you that earlier."

"You were busy engaging in fisticuffs. I'm fine." He settled his face against her fragrant hair and allowed his body to relax. "I'm sorry I made you faint."

"You didn't have to kill that man," she said softly.

He tightened his hold. "I explained that. Anybody tries to harm you, they die." It really was that simple, and he wasn't going to waver. "I'm not asking you to like that fact, but you are going to have to accept it."

"You're not a pirate any longer," she muttered.

What did any of that have to do with being a pirate? "I know. Or I'd still walk around with my sword." Truth be told, he missed his sword. Maybe they'd come back in style at some point.

She chuckled. "Your sword."

He smiled and tugged her onto her back. Her dark eyes were somehow luminous in the night, and a tinge of sadness echoed in them. "What's wrong?" he murmured, skimming his thumbs along her cheekbones.

She just shook her head.

"I can't fix it if I don't know what's bothering you," he said quietly.

"You can't fix everything." She reached up and brushed hair away from his face.

He studied her, trying to figure her out. It would probably take an eternity to understand the woman. "Are you injured? Hurt from the fight with Ginny?"

She rolled those eyes. "Of course not. Like I said, I was winning."

Yet he could feel her turmoil and sadness roll under his skin. "Talk to me."

"Enough talking." She pulled him down, her mouth seeking his. Her lips molded to his, and his body leaped to life.

A knock echoed on the door. Damn it. "What?" he asked, partially turning.

"It's Theo. I have something on Saul Libscombe."

Jared growled. His brother had always had such great timing. He pressed a kiss to Veronica's nose. "Get some sleep. I'll be back." Grousing, he shoved from the bed and yanked his jeans on, stomping barefoot into the hallway.

Theo snorted, his grin full of smart-ass as he handed over a stack of papers. "A couple of things. I hacked into Saul's finances, and there are some interesting withdrawals and moves against Uncle Benny. In addition, we've been hacked as well."

Jared's chin lowered. "We've been hacked?"

"The family holdings have been. Chalton is trying to backtrack to see who's been investigating us." Theo glanced toward the nearest window, where dawn was finally creeping over the hill. "I haven't slept." Turning on a combat boot, he strode down the hallway and pushed open a bedroom door.

Jared watched him go. What the hell? He sighed. Might as well go through the documents now, considering it was almost morning time anyway. Veronica needed sleep, and if he returned to the bedroom, that wasn't going to happen.

He read through the documents as he walked down the stairs and into the living room. A computer was already booted up, so he jumped on and started tracing through his family financials.

Hours later, a sound by the door caught his attention.

"Jared." Ginny looked up from her phone as she swept into the room. She wore a long blue skirt, frilly white shirt, and a ribbon in her full hair.

He paused, taken back to a time centuries ago. "You're up early."

She shrugged a small shoulder. "I'm unable to sleep and thought I'd read a book on this phone. How clever is it that we can read on phones? Speak on phones that are portable?" Her gaze caught on his bare chest.

Sometimes he forgot how things were before modern conveniences. "True." He should've put a shirt on. "I, ah—"

She smiled, showing her beauty, and moved inside to sit on the settee. "We've been avoiding a chat."

He winced and stood from the computer chair to stretch his aching neck. "I don't want to hurt you, Ginny. I really don't." Taking a seat next to her, he tried to think of a nice way to put his thoughts into words. "You meant the world to me so long ago." Yet had she? Had he built her up over the years just to keep himself unattached?

She laughed, the sound high and tinkly, like bells. "That was past tense, my friend." Looking his way, amusement filled her eyes. "I liked you, too."

He returned her smile. "I'm sorry you lost your mate."

"Me, too." She sobered. "I'm glad you've found yours. You have, right?"

He rubbed his chest. "Yes. I've found mine." So quickly, he found himself planning a life with Veronica. "She's everything I never knew I wanted. Needed." He'd spend eternity making her happy, and they had that now. He could court her like she deserved.

Ginny sighed and laid her head on his shoulder. "I'm so glad." Her voice was soft and a little wistful.

He patted her arm. "You'll find somebody to love, Ginny. I promise."

"Forget love. I just want freedom," she murmured with a deep sigh.

He frowned. "What do you mean?"

She turned then, her head still on his arm. "Modern life away from family and duty, of course."

Yeah. Of course.

Chapter 10

Ronni stopped short at seeing Ginny with her head on Jared's shoulder. A blade sliced through her chest, and she took a moment to roll her eyes at herself. Yeah, she'd fallen for the badass vampire, and who wouldn't? But he didn't owe her diddly squat.

She had to admit, with his size and Ginny's petite stature, they looked good. Dickheads.

Quietly stepping away from the living room, she made her way to the side entrance, her gun safe in her purse.

"Where are you going?" Olivia asked, looking up from the kitchen with a cup of coffee in her hand. Her eyes widened. "Are you kidding me? You got shot at yesterday and you're going back into the city."

Ronni's chin dropped. "I'm a cop, Olly. No way am I hiding out here and not solving Walt's murder. Seriously."

"You are not a cop," Olivia snapped, standing and reaching her.

Ronni shrugged. "Maybe not completely, but I've done the training." Sure, it was more for education and a bit of fun, but she wasn't some weak woman. "Nobody knows we're meeting this morning, and I need to find out what happened to Walt. He was a good guy, and I think we're close. I feel it."

Olivia shoved her coffee cup atop the clothes washing machine and grabbed her coat off a hook. "Fine. Let's go."

Ronni's eyebrows rose. "You aren't going."

Olivia got into her face. "I am going." Her eyes gleamed. "You asked me to be part of your little foursome of sleuths from the beginning, you know."

Yeah, because Olivia was a hell of an investigative journalist. Ronni gulped. "Won't Chalton be mad?"

"Yeah. He'll be mad," Olivia said with a bite. "So will Jared. You want to be an independent woman or not?"

"Hells, yeah." Ronni pulled open the door and ducked through swirling snow for the car. The wind pierced her sweater right to her skin, and she shivered, hurrying inside and igniting the engine.

Olivia jumped in next to her, scattering snow. "The storm is worse."

"Yeah." Ronni drove carefully away from the house, feeling like she was getting away with something. Take that, Jared. Fucking vampire.

Olivia cleared her throat. "What's going on, Ron?"

Ronni sighed. "Saw Jared and Ginny together in the living room."

Olivia winced. "Saw them doing what?"

"Just talking. Her head was on his shoulder." The image hurt, damn it.

"Just talking? Then who cares?" Olivia peered through the snow-filled windows. "Maybe we shouldn't drive in this."

Ronni continued down the long driveway. "I care. I mean, they have every right to talk, and it could've been innocent, but even so. He was in love with her centuries ago and never found anybody else. I don't think he even knows what he wants."

"You should ask him," Olivia said. "Help him figure it out."

"I know." Ronni blew out air. "Give me a break, Olly. Six days ago, I was next to death. Then I mate a vampire…which is the craziest thing ever. Somebody is trying to kill me, and I think I've fallen for said vampire. You can understand my not thinking all that clearly quite yet."

"I do understand." Olly nodded vigorously. "It all makes sense."

Ronni slowed by the gate as the trees swayed wildly around them. "We should probably stay here, right?" Sticking it to Jared with her show of independence didn't seem worth having a tree land on the car or a bullet hit her head. "This is reckless." She wasn't a stupid woman.

"Yeah. Maybe we can have the others come to us?" Olivia brushed snow off her jeans. "We could work the case from here. The coffee is excellent."

Ronni shuddered. "I've been trying to prove my worth for so

long, to my dad, that I have taken stupid chances." Or avoided risks. She was a shrink, for goodness' sake. "I understand my motivations."

"Sometimes hearing them out loud helps. You have nothing to prove to your father," Olivia said softly. "It's nice to see you finally realize that. Has Jared helped?"

"Maybe. I'm not sure. He treats me as something fragile but worthwhile at the same time." It was different than her father, that was for sure. As she let go of the past, her chest felt lighter.

"Good. I think that's good."

Ronni turned and grinned at her best friend. "You jumped in the car with me."

"Of course." Olivia smiled back. "I'm Thelma to your Louise. Monica to your Rachel. Tina Fey to your Amy Poehler." She turned to look out the back window. "You know, if you flip a quick U-turn, they'll never know we even left."

"Good plan." Ronni inched forward just as a massive vampire jumped over the car and landed in the road. She pushed the car into park. Jared stood there in the snow, legs braced, leather jacket over his bare chest. Boots covered his feet, and fury blanketed his rugged face. "Oh, crap."

He stomped forward and yanked open her door. He moved to sit down. "Scoot."

She scrambled to the center, pressing against Olivia. "Um..."

He turned, his eyes glittering black coal as he slammed the door. The spit dried up in her mouth. Then he jerked the gearshift into reverse.

Olivia leaned around Ronni, her blue eyes twinkling. "Jared, how kind of you to drive us back to the house. Ronni was just turning the car around."

Jared hit the gas pedal, and the car careened backward up the icy driveway.

Olivia cleared her throat. "I don't suppose we can keep Chalton out of this little adventure? What do you say, Jared?"

Jared turned and flashed her a smile that held absolutely no amusement. "I won't say a word."

Olivia breathed out, the sound relieved. "Good. That's good." She patted Ronni's leg as if in reassurance. Then she stiffened, craned her neck to look out the back window, and groaned. "He's at the back door."

Jared slid the vehicle under the carport and shut off the car.

Quiet ticked for the tiniest of seconds. Olivia's door was wrenched open.

Jared grabbed Ronni's arm and pulled her from the vehicle, rushing them both through the snowstorm and into the side entry.

She jerked free. "Enough."

He turned on her and slowly, way too deliberately, removed his leather jacket. "Where's your coat?"

She blinked. Her coat? "I forgot it."

"You forgot it. Again." He glowered over her, making her feel way too small and fragile.

"Yep." Forcing bravado, she ignored her racing heart and tried to brush past him.

He stopped her with a finger against her heart. "Did you or did you not get shot at last night?" His voice was a low rumble of mangled rebar mingled with shards of glass.

Her lungs seized. Okay. So he was really mad. "I have my gun."

"Your gun." He breathed out, tension pouring off him in waves. "You have your little shooter to handle another hit team with automatic weapons. Well shit, Veronica. I didn't know that."

She grimaced at the furious sarcasm. "You're overreacting."

Wrong thing to say. She knew it the second the last word left her mouth, but it was too late to grab it back.

Red flushed high and dark across Jared's sharp cheekbones. His nostrils flared. The atmosphere in the small room swelled with the force of his anger. "Is that a fact?" he growled.

Her legs trembled a second before her temper caught up. Thank God. She reared up, meeting his glittering gaze head on. "Yes. Plus, I didn't want to bother you. It seemed you and Ginny were deep into a cozy conversation, and you weren't even wearing a fucking shirt." Yeah, she sounded jealous. Who the hell cared? He had no right to be so furious at her.

His chin lowered.

Her stomach rolled.

"Listen, *mate*."

She held up a hand. "No. I'm done listening. You want that wallflower? That weak chick who needs you to tie her shoelaces? You can have her. I'm tired of it. Tired of you acting like we're all so breakable. Fuck off, Jared." Her words started to roll together so quickly she wasn't even sure what she said.

He stared at her.

Why the hell did he do that? It was as if he weighed every option, every decision…even in a temper. Finally, he seemed to reach a decision. "All right."

She shook her head. "What do you mean, all right?"

The slight curve of his lip held menace. "You don't want me to treat you as breakable?"

So much threat existed in the sentence, she had no choice but to instinctively deflect. "Jared, I'm so tired of your crap." In a suitable huff, she tried to move past him again.

And didn't make it.

Did he pick her up? No.

Toss her over his shoulder? No.

Instead, former pirate Jared Reese shot a hand into her hair, tangled, and pulled. He stormed through the kitchen and living room, his hold absolute.

She had no option but to follow along, considering her hair was nicely attached to her head, her face slightly down. "What the holy crap are you doing?" she hissed.

"Showing you," he snapped back, reaching the stairs.

She plowed a fist into his kidneys. "Showing me what? That you can drag a woman by the hair like a Neanderthal?"

He paused. "I'm not dragging you and you know it."

True. Yet she had no choice but to move. "You're showing me you're an ass."

"You already knew that." He twisted his wrist, and her head jerked back so her gaze could meet his. "What you apparently didn't know is that I can control you with one fucking hand. Just one. If that isn't the definition of breakable, I don't know what is." His fingers tightened just enough to hint pain along her scalp.

"You are such a dick." Which didn't explain why her nipples were peaking and her nerves firing. Did she actually like this side of him? Hell, no. So she punched out again.

His hand moved, faster than possible, to manacle around her neck. He jerked her face closer to his.

Her eyes widened.

"Back. Up." He enforced each word with his thumb against her jugular, pushing her just enough she had no choice but to lift her foot to the step behind her. "Again."

Okay. So he was making a good point, damn it. Her knees trembled in awareness as she was intrigued whether she wanted to be or not. "Let go of me or I'll just shoot you," she said, digging deep.

His chin lifted slightly. "Take the gun out."

Oops. It figured he'd accept that challenge.

"Fine." She reached behind her and tugged out the small pistol. One bullet wouldn't kill him.

He easily snagged the gun and tossed it over his shoulder.

Her mouth gaped open.

He glanced down and pressed a kiss—a very hard kiss—against her lips. Shocks cascaded through her, alighting fire to her every nerve.

"What is this? Vampire foreplay?" she gasped out.

"Yeah." His thumb tightened right under her jaw, and he lifted up. "Let's get a couple of things straight right now."

Even with her chin up, she could glance down at his jeans. "Looks like we already have."

His lips peeled away from his teeth. "What you saw earlier, what you should've interrupted earlier if it had bothered you, was me saying good-bye to Ginny."

Ronni's breath caught. "Good-bye. Out of duty, huh?"

"No." His eyes blazed. "I want you, Veronica. For my mate. Nobody else and certainly not her. Whatever was there was over centuries ago. You're my present and my future."

The sweet words were delivered with a hard edge. She swallowed. "Let go of my neck." She needed to think—away from him.

His hold tightened around her jugular. "No. We're settling this today. Go back."

She had no choice but to climb the steps backward, her gaze caught in the dark vortex of his. Before she knew it, she stood at the top. If she could just get the right leverage, she could shove his ass all the way down.

As if reading her thoughts, his lip quirked. "Centuries won't be enough to tame you," he rumbled.

"Damn straight—" She yelped as he stepped into her, his massive body backing her down the entire hallway to their bedroom. He could've easily picked her up and was still making his point. Her butt hit the door, and he reached around her to twist the knob.

"Inside." His voice lowered to guttural.

She swallowed and backed into the darkened bedroom. The storm raged outside, hiding the sun and casting a snowy gray glow through the quiet space. "I've had about enough—"

His mouth slammed down on hers. The firmness of his kiss was a shock that drove the oxygen from her lungs. There was no gentleness, no softness. Only fire and demand.

She'd seen the predator inside him.

This was the first time she *felt* it. Her own body responded as if she'd been sleeping her entire life and had just been shocked awake. The rush of energy cut through her with a blade of pain, narrowing the entire world to that second, to his touch, to Jared Reese.

The clarity brought on was too bright, too much, too everything.

She needed more. He'd chosen her, and she'd already done the same thing. Yet this edge to him kept her off balance, and she couldn't think.

Her whimper rolled up her chest and into his mouth.

He released her lips so she could pant frantically for breath. "You're gonna make that noise a lot today. Take off your clothes."

She tried to breathe, tried to fill her lungs. They compressed, pounding in time to the tingles along her skin, zapping her clit. No way could she give in so easily. "Make me."

This time, he gave her no warning. He flipped her around, wrapping an arm around her waist. "Gladly." He growled low, holding her in place and plunging his hand into her panties.

Her legs turned to rubber, barely holding her up.

He chuckled against her hair, his heated breath providing even more warning. With ruthless efficiency, he zeroed in on her clit. Sparks flew through her, making her ache.

Fire burned through the tiny nub as he rubbed and circled.

"Oh, God." She shut her eyes, leaning into him, trusting him to take her weight. His touch became her reality, and she gyrated against his talented fingers.

Smoother than possible, he flipped her around and took her mouth again, his tongue demanding entry, stroking in and out in perfect sync with his fingers on her clit.

She tried to rub against him, to open her legs wider, to get enough friction to fall over. More. She had to have more and now. It was too much and not enough at the same time. Lights flashed behind her eyes.

He pulled his hand away. "Oh, sweetheart. You're gonna beg before you come this time." Setting her away from him, he crossed his arms, leaning against the door. His eyes glittered, and a flush wound over his cheekbones. Dominance stamped hard on his face, rolling off him in a tension she could feel against her skin. "I told you to take off your clothes."

Chapter 11

Jared could smell her. The arousal, the desire, the fire-spitting woman.

His.

Oh, he'd been gentle with her, but that was over. He could lie to himself that he wanted to tame her, to make her submit, in order to gain her obedience in battle just to keep her safe from danger.

That'd be a fucking lie.

He wanted her submission, period. And he'd get it.

She knew it as well as he did—he could see it in her eyes. But he was gonna have to work for it.

Gladly.

She was smart and strong, and he liked that. He craved that. But right now, she was going to beg. "Now, Veronica," he murmured, easily standing between her and any freedom.

By the desire lighting her bourbon-colored eyes on fire, she didn't want freedom.

Good fucking thing.

Then challenge and defiance mingled with the desire. Keeping his gaze, she yanked her sweater off to leave her nearly see-through blouse. Then she slowly, very slowly, unbuttoned each delicate button. Her lip curled.

"Oh, baby," he whispered, heat roaring through his chest. "Don't push."

Her chin lowered, and she dropped her shirt to the floor. Her bra followed. Then her hands went to the clasp of her jeans.

He stopped breathing. The blood pounded through his ears.

She turned her back to him.

His head snapped against the door.

Slightly leaning over, she shimmied out of the jeans and panties, her spectacular ass swaying with each movement.

His cock pounded in his jeans, threatening to end things right then and there. Oh, then the wild woman would know she owned him. Not a chance in hell. His body undulated, his muscles vibrating, needing to tackle her onto the bed.

He used every bit of control he'd ever honed and forced his body to relax against the door. "Turn around." His breath was so heated, it hurt to speak.

She did so, her long hair brushing out. Her chin lifted. "What now?" she asked, her voice a throaty echo.

Christ, she was beautiful. Still a little too thin, but he could see her curves already coming back. Her angled features were all fiery Colombian, where her people came from. Smooth skin, full breasts, long legs. Fire and spirit, that was his woman. Icy-hot lust cut through him, landing hard in his balls. But this was a battle he fully intended to win. "Undress me," he said.

Her eyes gleamed. She might as well have screamed *challenge accepted*. Humming softly, she sauntered toward him, more dangerous than most of his enemies on earth. She licked her lips.

He bit down a groan.

The pads of her fingers brushed his abdomen as she pulled his leather jacket free, having to stand on her tiptoes to reach the collar. Then, just to attempt to kill him, she dropped to her knees.

Holy fuck.

He swallowed, tension spreading his legs wide.

She leaned in and unzipped his jeans. His cock sprang free, and she gave a throaty laugh. Her long hair caressed his dick as she painstakingly shoved his jeans to the ground.

He couldn't help it. His hand shaking, he speared his fingers through her hair and tugged her to her feet, kicking off his boots and jeans at the same time.

She jerked against his hold, her smile feminine and triumphant.

God, she was something. Amazing.

He planted a hand across her upper chest, spreading his fingers out. "What were you thinking, leaving the safety of this house earlier?"

Her pretty nipples, light brown and erect, all but begged for his mouth. She didn't answer.

That wouldn't do. He slid his hand down to palm a breast. She sucked in air, the muscles in her abdomen clenching hard enough he could see them work. Her swallow moved her entire throat. "I didn't think it all through," she admitted.

He indulged himself, leaning down to swirl his tongue around her other nipple. "Good girl." Honesty was good for them both. He lightly bit down.

The sound she gave shot right to his cock.

Then he dropped to his knees, kissing her torso on the way down. "Don't do it again." Grabbing both globes of her ass, he dug in his fingers and placed a gentle kiss against her mound.

Her legs trembled against his chest. Her scent drove him crazy. Drawing her in, he slowly licked her slit. If heaven had a taste, it was her. When he reached her clit, her knees buckled.

He picked her up, his hands still on her ass, and set her on the bed, still on his knees.

"You're so strong," she moaned.

Yeah. Vampire. He spread her legs wide and ran his palms along her inner thighs. They vibrated against his skin, so much need in the movement he could feel it in his own body. "Beautiful. You're the most beautiful woman I've ever seen, Veronica."

"Wh-why do you always call me that?" she whispered, lust in the tone.

"It's your name. I like it. Feminine, spunky, and charming." He leaned in and licked her again, humming as pleasure exploded inside him from the sweet contact. "Ronni is a cute tomboy playing baseball. Veronica is all woman—my woman." He nipped her clit.

She came off the bed, her cry strangled.

He could only torture them both for so long. "You need to know. I'm biting you today. The way I want to. You'll wear my marks for eternity, and they won't be faint. No confusion. You'll know every time you fucking see them who you belong to." Before she could answer, he slid his fangs into her thigh.

She cried out, arching.

Her blood filled his mouth, sweet and spicy. The primal being at his core rumbled wide awake, seeking and hunting. Yeah. He licked the wound closed, healing it until two puncture marks remained. "That's the first one."

She mumbled something, her body primed and ready.

So he went at her with his mouth, his tongue, his fingers. Touching her everywhere, keeping her on the edge, working every erogenous zone she had. Her taste tempted him, her scent surrounded him. But her cries, her sighs...they fulfilled him.

He lost himself in the texture and pleasure she offered. He took. He gave. Several times she tried to clamp her thighs together, to seek some sort of control or relief, and he kept her wide open.

For him.

Finally, a rush of energy zipped through her. He could feel it. There was no way to stop the orgasm about to take her, so he made it as good as he could. He plunged two fingers inside her, plucked one nipple, and sucked her entire clit into his heated mouth.

She screamed.

He grinned against her heated flesh, having no doubt her cry echoed throughout the entire house. Nothing in him cared even the slightest. They all knew she belonged to him. One cry merely confirmed that.

She whimpered, sweat coating her torso, and softened onto the bed.

He placed one last kiss against her core.

She twitched.

He stood and looked down at her. Slumbering eyes, relaxed jaw, satisfied expression. Good.

"That almost killed me." The sweetest smile he'd ever seen curved her full lips. "But I didn't beg," she hitched out.

He met her smile, his body on fire, his heart nearly exploding for her. It had happened quickly, but there was no doubt in his body, in his soul, that he fucking loved her. Would forever. "We're just getting started." Sliding a hand beneath her ass, he flipped her over and yanked her onto all fours. "Hold on, baby."

* * * *

Ronni's hair brushed forward, and she dug her nails into the bedspread to keep from flattening out again. Snow piled against the window, while a heated vampire stood behind her. Her body hummed, satisfied with electrical jolts still zipping through. Her eyelids were heavy, and she needed a nap.

But after the spectacular, more than amazing orgasm he'd just given her, the least she could do was hold still for a moment while he took his.

She sighed and let her body relax.

His fingers curled into her buttocks, catching her attention ever so slightly. There was no way she could go again. Maybe ever. So she wiggled her butt to entice him. "No need to wait." She was more than wet enough to take him, even with his size.

He slid a hand between her thighs.

Her body jerked as if she'd been shocked. Her well-loved sex clenched, and nearly painful sparks flew from her core. "I, ah, can't." She tried to rock forward and away from his hand.

His other hand flattened across her ass and held her in place. He leaned over her, his lips brushing her bare shoulder, one finger slowly entering her swollen tissues. "You can. You will. Every damn time."

She blinked. "Huh?"

"If I'm there, you're there." His fang nipped the shell of her ear.

Warmth unfolded inside her like a heater had just been turned on. "Jared, be realistic."

"I wasn't asking." His fingers pulled on her labia.

Her body trembled. Surprise turned to shock and flashed right to desire. How did he do that? "I, ah—"

He reached around and gently tugged on her breast. "You what, baby?" His rough voice had as much affect, as did his calloused fingers.

She shut her eyes, trying to get a handle on her rioting body. Every nerve flayed open, just like he wanted. Oh, she was tough and mentally strong, but every cell in her knew the vampire was stronger. Why that turned her on even more, she'd never understand. "Please—"

"Shhh. It's too early to beg." He licked along her earlobe as his hand released her breast to skim up and grasp the front of her neck.

"What is it with you and my neck?" she gasped.

With two fingers beneath her jaw, he applied pressure.

Her head lifted, her shoulders straightened, and her spine

elongated, arching her back. Her ass was up, displayed for him. Oh. Two fingers, and he did control her. Waves rolled through her, heavy with need.

He slapped her inner thighs. "Wider."

Oh, God. So much for him being too gentle. When she didn't comply fast enough, he flicked his wrist and tapped a finger against her clit. Hard.

Her cry was strangled, and her womb convulsed.

She wanted to drop her head down but his hold was absolute. Two fucking fingers.

He tapped her again, this time with a harder edge.

She hissed as need overwhelmed her. Going purely on instinct, she widened her thighs.

Not giving an inch, he slowly began to penetrate her, his cock harder than rock, stretching her to accommodate him. She bit her lip against the excruciating pleasure. She was completely open to him, to anything he chose to do to her. The helplessness, the shocking sense of being taken over, stole any thought she had to fight him.

It was all too wonderful. Oh, she should seek caution, but at the moment, her body ruled.

He overtook the atmosphere with determination and strength, controlling them both as he slid inside her, inch by deliberate inch. How was he even real? Tension cascaded off him along with heat, hinting at what it cost him. Yet he didn't waver.

She tightened her internal muscles, rippling around him.

He growled low but didn't pause or speed up.

Whoa. He was incredible. Not even remotely human, and it showed. And he was hers.

He lifted her head even more just as the last inch shoved inside, his balls to her ass.

She whimpered again, trying to get him moving.

"Now comes the begging," he murmured against her ear, the sound dark.

Fine. Whatever. She didn't care. "Please." Just move, damn it. "I'll do anything, Jared. Just move. Please."

"Excellent." He stiffened around her. "This is going to hurt more than your thigh and more than last time, Veronica." Not giving her a chance to question, he struck into the soft tissue where her neck met her shoulder, the same spot as before, his fangs slashing deep and imbedding in bone.

Pain ripped through her torso. She jolted and screamed, tears filling her eyes.

He grabbed her hip and withdrew, slamming home hard.

Sparks flashed behind her eyes. Her body convulsed. Need rippled through her to pierce beneath her skin. It was too much. His fangs didn't retract. A tear slid down her face. It was a claiming, brutal and primitive.

He slid out and pounded back in, setting up a hard rhythm that rocked the bed against the wall with loud bangs. But he held her in place with two fingers and twin fangs.

She could do nothing but accept it all. It was submission on a level she hadn't understood, and yet, she craved more. "Harder," she murmured. "More, Jared." Whatever he had, whoever he was, she wanted it all. Wanted to claim him in a way she barely understood.

He gave it to her.

Holding nothing back, he hammered into her, shooting her body into places she had never even imagined. She broke with a sharp cry, riding out the waves, whimpering at the end.

He didn't stop.

If anything, his speed and strength increased. Minutes later, maybe hours, she exploded again, his name the only sound on her lips. The third time, he was the only thing in her universe.

He held her close, shuddering with her this time.

She gasped, pleasure and pain pouring through her. Finally, he released her shoulder, licking until it stopped bleeding and the agonizing burning numbed. Her eyelids fluttered open to see it getting dark outside.

He withdrew and flipped her around to her back, allowing her to finally lie down before covering her, pressing back inside. She sighed in relief before her mind caught up. How in the world was he still hard?

She shook her head against the pillow. Her body didn't even feel like hers any longer. Over-sensitized to the point of still being needy, she wasn't sure of anything except him. Only him. Now that was power. "I, ah, can't," she mumbled, taking in his implacable face. "Not again."

He smiled. "Wanna bet?"

Chapter 12

Jared listened to the sleet slash against the window as the world moved outside without them, his arm around a soundly sleeping Veronica. They'd been in bed nearly twenty-four hours, but he had gotten up a couple of times to grab food.

He fingered the sharp bite marks and surrounding bruise on her neck. Even the healing properties from his saliva hadn't banished the bruise after he'd claimed her. After the first several hours, he'd lost count of how many times she screamed his name while pleasure took her under. He fucking loved that sound. Who knew he'd find his perfect wild match in an arranged mating?

Did fate really have a plan?

Truth be told, he didn't give a damn. Veronica was his, fate or not.

A rap echoed on his door. He frowned. Reality was bound to intrude at some point. Gently moving Veronica to the side, he covered her with the blankets and moved from the bed to yank his jeans up.

He padded barefoot to open the door. "What?" he growled.

"You're not going to believe this," Theo spat, fury rolling off him.

Jared moved into the hallway and shut the door, following his brother down to the kitchen. "What's going on?" A quick glance at the clock confirmed it was nearly noon. Time flied when one was fucking within an inch of one's life. He grinned.

Theo whirled on him.

Jared lost the smile and went on full alert. Were they in danger? "Spit it out, Theo."

Chalton moved in from the living room, munching on a sandwich.

"Holy shit, brother. Does your dick still work?"

Jared frowned at him. "Jealous?"

"No. You probably need talcum powder or something," Chalton said cheerfully. "Glad you worked it out with your mate."

Jared grinned. "Me, too."

Chalton glanced at Theo. "Whoa. What crawled up your butt?"

Theo sucked in air, his nostrils flaring. "The hack into our system. I found the hacker."

Jared's eyebrows rose. "That's good."

"Is it? Is it, Jared?" Theo snapped, putting his hands on his hips.

Jared cocked his head to the side. What the hell was wrong with Theo? "Yes?" he asked.

"No. I mean, no. Damn it. Don't you see?" Theo threw up his hands. "She shows up, out of the blue, and right now? Right when everything is going to shit around us?"

"Uh." Jared rubbed his whiskers, trying to decipher the sentence. "Who, Theo?"

"Ginny." Theo's eyes spit black fire. "Right now, she just shows up?"

"Ginny?" Jared glanced at Chalton and back. "I figured maybe she heard about the mating and showed up."

"No," Theo said lowly. "She hacked us. She took the Benjamin file with her. Printed the whole thing out, bleached the hard drive, and took it."

Jared reared back. "Ginny? No way."

"Yes, way," Theo bellowed. "You have always had a blind spot for that manipulative bitch. Jesus. She was here for a reason, and she took the Benjamin file."

"That's crazy," Chalton breathed.

The Benjamin file was a complete list of all their holdings, real and personal property—as well as family dynamics and secrets they didn't want out. "Why?" Jared asked. "What did she want?"

"I don't know. The more important question is who she's working for," Theo said grimly. He glanced at the phone in his hand. "I have a lead on her, and I'm tracking her down."

Jared paused. "Should I do that?"

"No." Theo said, his eyes gleaming. "You deal with your woman. I'll handle this one." He grabbed his jacket and stomped out of the room.

Jared's mouth dropped open. "Theo and Ginny?"

Chalton shook his head. "He's going to kill her. Know any good lawyers?"

Jared scrubbed both hands down his face. "We have to figure this out." Voices from the other room caught his attention. "Who's here?"

"Veronica's crime-fighting unit that was supposed to meet yesterday morning." Chalton grinned. "Before your marathon that included all of us hearing your name screamed a lot more than I ever wanted."

Jared rolled his eyes, his brain returning instantly to the threat at hand. "I'll awaken Veronica. We need to kill the person who poisoned her before going after Ginny."

"One disaster at a time," Chalton agreed easily. "Everyone is just eating right now, but I think the doctor has news she's ready to share."

"All right." Jared pivoted and headed back upstairs. He opened the bedroom door to see Veronica still sleeping peacefully, her face turned toward him. She was sweet and fragile in sleep, and he had to fight the urge to crawl back into bed with her and sleep the stormy day away. "Veronica." He reached her and gently shook her shoulder.

Her eyelids fluttered open. "What?" she muttered.

He grinned. The woman was a grump. "Your friends are here. Downstairs."

"Don't care." She stretched like a lazy cat and shut her eyes. "Tired."

He had made the second mating a marathon, now hadn't he? "Okay. You stay here and sleep, and I'll talk to them."

Her eyelids flashed open. Realization dawned, and she sat up, holding the blankets to her chest. "No." She shook her head, and that glorious hair splayed down her bare back. "I forgot about the case for a moment."

Masculine pride puffed out his chest.

She rolled her eyes. "Get over yourself." Pushing across the bed, she put distance between them. Then she groaned as she stood.

"Sore?" he asked mildly.

She glared over her bruised shoulder. "Nope. Not at all."

"We'll see what we can do about that later, then."

* * * *

Ronni finished dressing in a thick sweater and her faded jeans after a very hot shower, her entire body aching with an annoying set of tingles. Every time her legs moved, her sex clenched, and she fought a moan.

There wasn't an inch of her that hadn't been caressed, licked, or explored by Jared. The man, the *male*, had found nerves she hadn't known existed.

Everywhere.

Her breasts felt heavy and full in the bra, and she wanted nothing better than to shrug out of the thing.

Instead, she slapped a smile on her face and gingerly made her way downstairs to the main living room. Mabel and Lance sat on the sofa, Olivia shared the love seat with Chalton, while Jared leaned against the doorframe, distrust darkening his features. Papers and manila files were scattered across the sofa table.

Mabel looked up, her blue eyes lightening with her smile. "Hi, there. Feeling better?"

Ronni caught herself. Heat filled her face. "Ah, well—"

"From the poisoning," Olivia hastened to say. "I was just telling Mabel that it looks like your body fought the poison, and you're going to be all right."

Oh. Of course Mabel didn't have a clue about the sex marathon. Ronni's cheeks hurt, but she forced her smile wider. "Yes. I'm feeling much better."

Lance narrowed his gaze in his detective look. "Are you sure? You're moving funny."

Jared coughed into his hand.

Ronni shot him a look. "I'm fine. Slipped on the ice earlier."

"Come sit down." Mabel patted the place next to her. "You're not going to believe this. I found the original autopsy report on Walt, and there were contusions, showing he fought somebody right before death."

Lance hissed out a breath and plunked his badge on the sofa. "Not going to need this."

"Yes, you are," Mabel countered, shoving her dark hair away from her pretty face. "We're doing this the right way. You put that back."

Lance stared at her for a moment and then slowly retrieved his badge.

"Good. There was also a puncture wound under the detective's neck," Mabel said, pointing to a series of pictures scattered on the papers. "He was definitely murdered."

"Dr. Counts is in on it. Or he was bribed," Lance said, fury in his voice.

Olivia nodded. "That makes sense, right? I mean, as a coroner with a medical degree, he'd know plenty about exotic poisons. Well, probably."

Ronni gulped. "Yeah, and he hangs out at the cop bar as well as in our office sometimes. If he really wanted to poison me, it wouldn't have been too difficult."

"What does he have to do with missing drugs from lockup?" Lance asked grimly.

Who knew?

Chalton reached for a stack of papers. "We're going through all the financials now, trying to find any sort of link to anybody. Nothing yet."

Ronni grabbed a yellow pad of paper. "All right. I'll go through this stack."

Jared straightened. "The weather has finally let up, so I'm going to scout the property for threats." He gestured for Ronni to follow him.

She frowned and did so, reaching the kitchen.

He brushed hair away from her face, his eyes warm. "You are moving stiffly. Are you all right?"

Warmth filtered through her chest. "I like all sides of you," she murmured, leaning up to place a kiss on his hard chin.

One of his dark eyebrows rose. "I have sides?"

"Yeah. Hard and tough. Sweet and gentle. Passionate and wild." She couldn't remember her life before him, and really, she'd just met him. That had to mean something big.

He grinned. "You've got a real sweet side, too. Stay inside, and holler if you guys find anything."

She'd forgotten bossy and arrogant. Oh, well. For now, she had a job to do. Turning back, she bit down a yelp as he smacked her on the ass. Oh, he'd pay for that later. She chuckled. Yeah. Fun and crazy. He was those things, too.

* * * *

Jared finished cleaning his gun, his gaze on the gathering storm outside. While the weather had finally broken and provided sun on sparkling snow for a few hours, the next round of snow and wind was rapidly arriving with the night.

An itch set up between his shoulder blades.

Veronica and her pals were still working away in the living room, while Chalton was hacking files left and right with his computer—mainly investigating the two other people in the living room. Detective Lance Peters and Dr. Mabel Louis didn't get a pass, just because Veronica and Olivia liked them. Jared had scouted the area outside and now was left with nothing to do.

Oh, he could go through the papers with the rest of them, but somebody had to take watch, and he was the most experienced.

He shrugged off unease. Having a mate in danger no doubt added tension to a guy's psyche, and as soon as he took care of the threat, he'd feel much better. As would she. While she kept up a brave front, he could tell it cost her. The fact that somebody had actually wanted her dead.

It was a sobering thought.

He polished the barrel of his gun, wondering if he should get one of the green laser guns out of the safe in the basement. Those would deal with immortals as well as humans.

The lights went out.

He stiffened and stood, listening. Wind blew through the world outside, scattering sleet and ice.

A couple of flashlights ignited from the living room, and the sound of a lighter echoed. Candlelight followed the flashlights.

"Think it's the storm?" Chalton asked, reaching the doorway.

Tension clawed through Jared. "No. Everybody get down." He'd barely bellowed the order when red laser beams pierced through the windows. "Veronica," he yelled, jumping for the living room.

He landed on his knees and skidded inside. Volleys of bullets pinged through the windows, shattering glass in every direction. Olivia screamed, and Chalton tackled her to the floor. Bullets hit the sofas and chairs, spewing cotton filling everywhere.

Jared reached Veronica just as Mabel pulled Lance away from the window. The cop yanked his gun from his waistband and crab walked toward the far window.

"Shit," Chalton snapped. "Holy fuck. Benny is going to kill us. This was my last chance, Jared. After the apartment in the city—"

Jared's chest heated. "One threat at a time," he snarled. Yeah, Benny would kill them for allowing his house to be trashed—especially after the whole penthouse debacle. Probably with a great deal of pain and some fire. Ben loved fire. For now, they had to take care of the attackers outside. "How many do you think?" He crouched on the floor, Veronica at his side.

"At least three," Detective Lance said, inching closer to the wall. "They must've followed us here. I haven't asked. Do you guys know what you're doing?"

Considering they had four centuries of battle and fighting on the detective, probably fucking yes. "We do," Jared said calmly. His temper rioted, and his need for vengeance tasted like blood. The cowards shooting from the tree line were aiming at his woman. "We, however, don't arrest the enemy." They killed.

The detective looked at him, his gaze sober. "No problem."

They were on the same page then.

Mabel drew a nine mil from her jacket. "They have to know we're armed."

True. Jared frowned.

Canisters crashed through the windows, and gas started to spew.

"Gas," the detective yelled. "Get out of the room."

Veronica started coughing, her eyes panicked. Jared grabbed the back of her neck and dragged her toward the kitchen.

She was right. It was always her neck.

Chapter 13

Ronni's eyes stung, and her lungs felt like she'd swallowed smoldering cigarette ashes. "What is that?" she gasped, stumbling for the kitchen.

"Tear gas," Jared said, one arm around her torso as he helped her along, his gun out and ready. "It doesn't bother us as much as you, and I can still see. We need to get you to the basement."

"What if they have explosives?" Chalton hissed from right behind her.

More bullets sprayed through the windows, and Jared pulled her toward the ground.

She ducked, closing her eyes, coughing out in agony. Static buzzed between her ears. She couldn't breathe. Panic swept ice along her skin, and she trembled. Her gun was upstairs.

Lance yelled in pain, crashing into the table. Blood spurted from his left arm. "Damn bastard," he hissed, his dark skin going pale.

Jared set Ronni against the fridge. "Stay here." He crept low to reach Lance, grabbing the detective's shirt, protecting his head from flying debris. "Need to apply pressure." Glancing around, he took a dishtowel off the counter to tie around the wound.

Lance groaned and lifted his gun to the kitchen door. "They'll be coming in."

More gunfire echoed, and glass flew all around them.

Two more canisters barreled in to bounce along the hard tile.

"Flash grenades." Jared pivoted and covered Ronni with his body.

Something exploded. Her skull rocked against his chest, and her vision blurred. Her central nervous system hitched. She blinked, trying to concentrate, a buzzing filling her head. "Wh-what?" she breathed.

He leaned back, his face blurry. "Flash grenade," he yelled.

She couldn't concentrate. Her chest hurt. "Jared." Tears filled her eyes.

"It's okay," he whispered in her ear, hunching over her and scooting her toward a door near the utility room. "Panic room downstairs. Lock yourself in." He motioned for Chalton over his shoulder.

He pulled open the door, and wooden steps came into view. Before Ronni could descend, a crash came from the front of the house.

Then the back door careened open, bouncing off the hall and hanging drunkenly.

Jared shoved his gun into her hand. "Shoot if necessary. Go. Now."

Ronni reached for Olivia, who had blood sliding from her nose. "Olly?"

Olivia grasped the railing, her face pale, her eyes unfocused.

"It's okay." Ronni gently sent her walking down, her movements hitched. She looked up just as Mabel slid her way on her knees.

Mabel coughed uncontrollably, moving into the stairwell. "My gun is under the table. I dropped it after the flash grenade." Her left eye was rapidly swelling, and blood poured from a cut above it.

Ronni ripped off a piece of her shirt. "Press that."

Mabel nodded and moved to help Olivia down the stairs.

"Panic room at the bottom," Ronni said, the gun heavy in her hand. Her vision cleared, and her body centered. She wasn't a cop, but she'd trained with many of them. Ducking down, she twisted her body to see beyond the door.

Lance reared up by the sink and fired rapidly through the glass.

Jared plowed into a man wearing all black, both of them careening into the utility room and out of sight.

"Jared!" Ronni called, half lifting on the stairwell. The sound of punches and grunts competed with the sparking toaster filled with bullet holes.

Lance cried out and fell hard, his head bouncing off the tile.

"Lance!" Ronni crawled toward him, glass cutting into her hands, even with the gun in one. She reached him. Blood arced from his temple. She planted a hand on his chest to feel it moving. Good. That was good. A bullet appeared to have sliced his forehead, but there wasn't a hole.

She looked up.

Chalton fought hand to hand with a man in all black in the living room, the two throwing furious kicks. A chair spun out of their way.

She swallowed.

Another gunman started firing outside the kitchen, hitting the table above her head.

She yelped, her chest heating. Slapping the gun into her waistband, she manacled Lance's shirt and pulled him toward the basement. "Mabel?" she yelled.

Mabel rushed up from the bottom, her eyebrow still bleeding, her eye all the way closed. "Can't see very well." The coroner frowned, and panic mangled her expression when she saw Lance. "Oh, God. Is he—"

"Just knocked out." Ronni grunted as she pulled his body down two stairs.

Mabel breathed out and cradled his head. "Let's get him to the panic room." She half-stood, keeping his head from the steps.

Ronni lifted his feet the best she could, and they hurried in getting him downstairs, bumping his shoulders and butt on the way down. She winced. He was too heavy for them to completely lift.

They reached the bottom and dragged him into a large cement room complete with a couple of beds, canned food, and dead computer consoles. Olivia pushed off the floor and moved their way, her gaze still dazed.

Ronni looked around. "See if you can get the computers running. There are probably cameras."

Mabel set Lance's head down gently. "On it. I can't see very well, Ronni. My vision is really fuzzy."

"Probably a concussion." Ronni patted her arm. "Stay here, and lock the door if it seems like the gunmen are making their way down here." The door was a thick steel and looked like it belonged on a bank vault. "Take care of Olly and Lance." She drew out her gun and ran up the stairs.

Reaching the top, she crouched and angled the gun outside.

Jared flew by in a hard tackle, smashing a man into the kitchen table. The heavy wood gave, splintering to the ground.

Another man in all black, his face covered, swung inside from the utility room. He pointed his gun at the back of Jared's head.

"Jared!" Ronni screamed, taking aim and firing.

* * * *

Jared felt a bullet whiz by his head on the heels of Veronica's scream.

He rolled off the guy he'd tackled, sending pieces of the table spinning across the floor. The guy groaned and punched him in the temple. Stars exploded across his vision.

His fangs dropped, and his temper flew.

With a growl, he shoved both fingers up the man's neck, twisted, and pulled back.

Blood sprayed to cover him.

He threw the guy's larynx and trachea across the room along with muscle, tissue, and a shitload of blood. The mass landed with a squishy pop against the cupboards. The corpse flopped twice and then went silent. Rolling back on his shoulders, Jared launched himself to his feet.

Turning, he paused at seeing Veronica's stark pale face. Shock widened her pupils as she stared at the dead man on the ground. The mask over his face still covered him to the nose, but a gaping bloody hole remained where his throat had been.

She swallowed. "Ah."

"You shot me." A man jerked round the door and grabbed her up. "Bitch."

Jared stilled. Something crashed in the living room. "Release her or..." He let the body on the floor finish his sentence.

The man held her tighter, blood spurting from his leg. His gun settled against her ribcage. "We're backing out of here. Now."

Her mouth dropped open and closed, her gun pointed down. She was definitely in shock. Yet her eyes focused, and her body straightened against the masked man holding her.

The guy was about six feet tall, and the knit mask covered him from the top of his head to his chin. Only his eyes, a deep blue, could be seen. "Move," he muttered.

Jared looked at the gun, at Veronica's wide eyes, at the bullet hole. He forced a grin. "You shot him?"

She rubbed soot off her chin. "He was aiming at you."

Ah. What a sweetheart. "Nice shot. He's gonna bleed out in no time." Well, maybe. The blood seemed to be ebbing a little. Maybe she hadn't hit a major artery.

The guy started pulling her toward the destroyed kitchen door.

"Let her go and I won't kill you," Jared said calmly, his peripheral vision catching Chalton staggering in from the other room to drop an unconscious man to the floor. It took a second, but he recognized the guy as the medical examiner from pictures he'd studied earlier that day. So Mabel had been correct. "Any more in there?" he asked his brother.

"One dead," Chalton breathed out, rolling his shoulders. "Kept this one alive."

"Good. He can answer questions." Jared kept his gaze on the man holding his woman and forced his fangs to retract. It wouldn't do to scare her any more than he already had. "Let Veronica go," he ordered again.

The man holding her didn't answer and instead kept dragging Veronica toward the door.

Jared leaped faster than a human could track, grabbed the gun, and yanked the barrel away from his woman. He spun her away and toward Chalton to catch.

Then he grabbed the man by the throat.

"Stop," Detective Lance said, staggering up the stairs. "Don't kill him."

Damn it.

"Please, Jared," Veronica whispered.

Ah, shit. Fine. He knocked the guy to the ground and ripped off the mask.

Lance gasped. "Lieutenant?"

Jared glanced at the man he'd only met once at the party. The retiring Lieutenant Smalt? Now this was interesting.

Chapter 14

Ronni huddled in a blanket on the ruined sofa, sipping a cup of coffee Jared had forced into her hands. Olivia sat next to her, doing the same thing. Chalton had an arm around Olivia, his feet up on the scratched and bullet-riddled coffee table.

The entire room was a mess of bullet holes, smashed glass, and destroyed furniture.

Police detectives and crime techs milled around, taking notes and pictures. Lance supervised the process, a bandage across his forehead and around his arm. Mabel gave her statement to yet another cop over in the corner.

Jared stood near the doorway, explaining once again how he'd ripped out the throat of the hired thug. Finally, he finished and moved her way to crouch in front of her. "We've been released. Let's get out of their way and go upstairs."

Lance walked toward them. "Is everybody all right?" he asked, his eyes weary.

"Yes," Ronni murmured. "The lieutenant? Seriously?"

Lance shook his head. "Apparently his retirement pension wasn't enough for him. He stole the drugs from lockup along with his partner in crime, the medical examiner."

Her stomach hurt. "So the lieutenant poisoned me. And killed Walt."

"Walt must've figured it out somehow." Lance sighed. "I'd bet the lieutenant did the actual killing. Unfortunately, he's not stupid. He's lawyered up."

Figured. "You'll get him, Lance." She forced a smile.

"Damn straight," Lance said, glancing over toward Mabel. "We have techs combing through his life right now."

"If you don't get him, I will," Jared said lowly.

Lance blinked. "I did not hear that." He turned to cross to Mabel, sliding an arm over her shoulders.

"They make a nice couple," Olivia mused, the color back in her pretty face.

Chalton sighed. "Do you think Benny knows about the house?"

Jared winced. "No. We're still alive."

Ronni glanced from one to the other. "Will your uncle really try to kill you?"

"Yes," they both answered.

"Well, that's unacceptable," she said, drawing the blanket around her aching body. "There has to be some way to appease him."

Jared ducked and lifted her into his arms, surrounding her with the sense of safety. Of security. Of something hot. "We'll figure something out. If nothing else, he'll want us breathing until we track down Ginny and the Benjamin file she stole."

Ronni settled against his chest, feeling safe for the first time in way too long. "The what?"

"File that holds all the information on our real and personal property. Bank codes, security codes...all tons of codes." Jared made his way up the stairs to their bedroom, his steps sure and steady. "We have hard copies of the files, so that's not the problem."

Ronni snuggled into his neck. "What's the problem?"

"Ginny, or whoever she's working for, can steal from us." He nudged the door open.

Ronni sighed, closing her eyes. "So you're loaded?"

"I do all right," he murmured. "Kept a lot of the bounty from my pirate days and then invested it."

Figured. Ronni grinned. "I knew there was more to Ginny than what we saw."

"I guess. I think Theo figured that out, too." Jared placed her on the bed and kicked the door shut. "That was a great shot you made earlier. Thanks for keeping me from being shot in the head."

She smiled and reached for him, cupping his whiskered jaw. "I kind of like your head."

"I love yours." He dropped to his knees, his hands on her thighs. "Though I should tell you that I love you. Everything about you. Am I'm so thankful fate brought us together."

Her heart heated and rolled right over. "You believe in fate?"

He shrugged. "Have to. You're too perfect, we're too good together, to just have been a fluke." He brushed her hair away from her face. "I'll spend eternity loving you, baby. Keeping you safe. And happy."

She already was. "I love you, too. You're everything I never knew I needed."

He grinned then. "Amen to that."

* * * *

Also from 1001 Dark Nights and Rebecca Zanetti, discover TEASED and TANGLED.

Sign up for the 1001 Dark Nights Newsletter
and be entered to win a Tiffany Key necklace.

There's a contest every month!

Go to www.1001DarkNights.com to subscribe.

As a bonus, all subscribers will receive a free
1001 Dark Nights story
The First Night
by Lexi Blake & M.J. Rose

Turn the page for a full list of the
1001 Dark Nights fabulous novellas...

Discover 1001 Dark Nights Collection Three

HIDDEN INK by Carrie Ann Ryan
A Montgomery Ink Novella

BLOOD ON THE BAYOU by Heather Graham
A Cafferty & Quinn Novella

SEARCHING FOR MINE by Jennifer Probst
A Searching For Novella

DANCE OF DESIRE by Christopher Rice

ROUGH RHYTHM by Tessa Bailey
A Made In Jersey Novella

DEVOTED by Lexi Blake
A Masters and Mercenaries Novella

Z by Larissa Ione
A Demonica Underworld Novella

FALLING UNDER YOU by Laurelin Paige
A Fixed Trilogy Novella

EASY FOR KEEPS by Kristen Proby
A Boudreaux Novella

UNCHAINED by Elisabeth Naughton
An Eternal Guardians Novella

HARD TO SERVE by Laura Kaye
A Hard Ink Novella

DRAGON FEVER by Donna Grant
A Dark Kings Novella

KAYDEN/SIMON by Alexandra Ivy/Laura Wright
A Bayou Heat Novella

STRUNG UP by Lorelei James
A Blacktop Cowboys® Novella

MIDNIGHT UNTAMED by Lara Adrian
A Midnight Breed Novella

TRICKED by Rebecca Zanetti
A Dark Protectors Novella

DIRTY WICKED by Shayla Black
A Wicked Lovers Novella

THE ONLY ONE by Lauren Blakely
A One Love Novella

SWEET SURRENDER by Liliana Hart
A MacKenzie Family Novella

For more information, visit www.1001DarkNights.com.

Discover 1001 Dark Nights Collection One

FOREVER WICKED by Shayla Black
CRIMSON TWILIGHT by Heather Graham
CAPTURED IN SURRENDER by Liliana Hart
SILENT BITE: A SCANGUARDS WEDDING by Tina Folsom
DUNGEON GAMES by Lexi Blake
AZAGOTH by Larissa Ione
NEED YOU NOW by Lisa Renee Jones
SHOW ME, BABY by Cherise Sinclair
ROPED IN by Lorelei James
TEMPTED BY MIDNIGHT by Lara Adrian
THE FLAME by Christopher Rice
CARESS OF DARKNESS by Julie Kenner

Also from 1001 Dark Nights

TAME ME by J. Kenner

For more information, visit www.1001DarkNights.com.

Discover 1001 Dark Nights Collection Two

WICKED WOLF by Carrie Ann Ryan
WHEN IRISH EYES ARE HAUNTING by Heather Graham
EASY WITH YOU by Kristen Proby
MASTER OF FREEDOM by Cherise Sinclair
CARESS OF PLEASURE by Julie Kenner
ADORED by Lexi Blake
HADES by Larissa Ione
RAVAGED by Elisabeth Naughton
DREAM OF YOU by Jennifer L. Armentrout
STRIPPED DOWN by Lorelei James
RAGE/KILLIAN by Alexandra Ivy/Laura Wright
DRAGON KING by Donna Grant
PURE WICKED by Shayla Black
HARD AS STEEL by Laura Kaye
STROKE OF MIDNIGHT by Lara Adrian
ALL HALLOWS EVE by Heather Graham
KISS THE FLAME by Christopher Rice
DARING HER LOVE by Melissa Foster
TEASED by Rebecca Zanetti
THE PROMISE OF SURRENDER by Liliana Hart

Also from 1001 Dark Nights

THE SURRENDER GATE By Christopher Rice
SERVICING THE TARGET By Cherise Sinclair
For more information, visit www.1001DarkNights.com.

About Rebecca Zanetti

Rebecca Zanetti is the author of over thirty romantic suspense and dark paranormal novels, and her books have appeared multiple times on the New York Times, USA Today, BnN, iTunes, and Amazon bestseller lists. She has received a Publisher's Weekly Starred Review for Wicked Edge, Romantic Times Reviewer Choice Nominations for Forgotten Sins and Sweet Revenge, and RT Top Picks for several of her novels. Amazon labeled Mercury Striking as one of the best romances of 2016 and Deadly Silence as one of the best romances in October. The Washington Post called Deadly Silence, "sexy and emotional." She believes strongly in luck, karma, and working her butt off…and she thinks one of the best things about being an author, unlike the lawyer she used to be, is that she can let the crazy out. Find Rebecca at: www.rebeccazanetti.com

Discover More Rebecca Zanetti

TEASED
A Dark Protectors Novella
By Rebecca Zanetti

The Hunter

For almost a century, the Realm's most deadly assassin, Chalton Reese, has left war and death in the past, turning instead to strategy, reason, and technology. His fingers, still stained with blood, now protect with a keyboard instead of a weapon. Until the vampire king sends him on one more mission; to hunt down a human female with the knowledge to destroy the Realm. A woman with eyes like emeralds, a brain to match his own, and a passion that might destroy them both—if the enemy on their heels doesn't do so first.

The Hunted

Olivia Roberts has foregone relationships with wimpy metro-sexuals in favor of pursuing a good story, bound and determined to uncover the truth, any truth. When her instincts start humming about missing proprietary information, she has no idea her search for a story will lead her to a ripped, sexy, and dangerous male beyond any human man. Setting aside the unbelievable fact that he's a vampire and she's his prey, she discovers that trusting him is the only chance they have to survive the danger stalking them both.

* * * *

TANGLED
A Dark Protectors Novella
By Rebecca Zanetti

Now that her mask has finally slipped…

Ginny O'Toole has spent a lifetime repaying her family's debt, and she's finally at the end of her servitude with one last job. Of course, it couldn't be easy. After stealing the computer files that will free her once and for all, she finds herself on the run from a pissed off vampire who has never fallen for her helpless act. A deadly predator too sexy for his own good. If he doesn't knock it off, he's going to see just how powerful she can really be.

He won't be satisfied until she's completely bare.

Theo Reese had been more than irritated at the beautiful yet helpless witch he'd known a century ago, thinking she was just useless fluff who enjoyed messing with men's heads. The second he discovers she's a ruthless thief determined to bring down his family, his blood burns and his interest peaks, sending his true nature into hunting mode. When he finds her, and he will, she'll understand the real meaning of helpless.

Deadly Silence
Blood Brothers, Book 1
Now Available

The first book in a breathtaking new romantic suspense series that will appeal to fans of *New York Times* bestsellers Maya Banks, Lisa Gardner, and Lisa Jackson.

DON'T LOOK BACK

Under siege. That's how Ryker Jones feels. The Lost Bastards Investigative Agency he opened up with his blood brothers has lost a client in a brutal way. The past he can't outrun is resurfacing, threatening to drag him down in the undertow. And the beautiful woman he's been trying to keep at arm's length is in danger...and he'll destroy anything *and* anyone to keep her safe.

Paralegal Zara Remington is in over her head. She's making risky moves at work by day and indulging in an affair with a darkly dangerous PI by night. There's a lot Ryker isn't telling her and the more she uncovers, the less she wants to know. But when all hell breaks loose, Ryker may be the only one to save her. If his past doesn't catch up to them first...

Full of twists and turns you won't see coming, DEADLY SILENCE is *New York Times* bestselling author Rebecca Zanetti at her suspenseful best.

* * * *

Ryker pushed back from the table, stood, and moved toward her. "This is a conversation better had where I can touch you." Dipping his shoulder, he lifted her in corded arms.

Zara yelped and grabbed his chest for balance. "What are you doing?" she whispered. How was he so strong? Even for a healthy guy who worked out, his strength was somehow beyond the norm. Fluid and natural.

He turned, grabbed his jacket, and strode for the living room, dropping onto her couch and setting those thick boots on her glass coffee table. The jacket had landed next to him. One arm remained beneath her knees and the other around her shoulders, easily cradling her against his rock-hard chest. His lips snapped over her jugular with just enough force to make her jump. Then, clearly indulging himself, he tugged the clip from her hair, which cascaded down. Burying his face in the mass of dark curls, he breathed in. "I love your hair."

She tried to perch primly on his lap and not snuggle right into him. His strength was as much of a draw as his passion. "What conversation did you want to have?"

He leaned back and waited until she'd turned her head to face him. "We agreed to keep this casual."

"I know." She played with a loose thread on his dark T-shirt.

"Then you started cooking me dinner."

She blinked. "I like to cook."

"Then you started keeping my beer on hand and lighting candles with every meal."

She shrugged. "Candles create nice light that helps with digestion." Could she sound like any more of a dork?

"Right." He played idly with her hair, heat from his body keeping her toasty warm.

Flutters awakened again throughout her body, and her nipples hardened. Good thing the bright red bra had plenty of padding. She tried to shift her weight, not surprised when he kept her easily in place. "I have not asked you for anything," she murmured, panic beginning to take hold.

"I like that about you." He punctuated the words with a tug on her hair. "In fact, I like you."

"I like you, too." The words, until now, had gone unsaid, but that's all they had, and that's all they were. It was an adventure, and she was truly enjoying the ride. She knew where they stood. "Stop playing with me."

"I'm not playing." His gaze dropped to her lips right before he leaned in to rest his mouth over hers.

Liquid fire shot from her chest to her sex.

He nibbled on her bottom lip, kissed the corners of her mouth, lightly whispering against her. "This is playing." The hand in her hair twisted, drawing back her head and elongating her neck. "This is not."

He swooped in, angled his mouth over hers, and took. Deep and hard, he kissed her, his mouth alone having enough power to drive her head back against his palm.

Hunger slammed through her, and she moaned low in her throat. Pleasure swamped her, head to toe, vibrating in waves as she kissed him back. Her nails dug into his chest, and she tried to move closer into him. He controlled the kiss, taking her deeper, his erection easily discernible beneath her butt.

Finally, he lifted his head, his eyes the color of a rocky riverbed beneath a stormy sky. "Who hit you?"

The simple words struck like a splash of cold water in the face. Shock dropped her mouth open. Had he been trying to manipulate her by kissing her like that? Sure, he'd been passionate with her many times, but something felt different. A wildness she'd always sensed in him seemed to be breaking free. "Forget you." Slamming her hand against his chest, she shoved off his lap.

"Zara." One word, perfectly controlled. He held up a hand, showing a long scar across his love line. One that he'd never explained, even when she'd asked nicely.

Her knees shook, but she backed away until her shoulders hit the fireplace mantel. Anger and panic welled up in her, and she couldn't separate them and think, so she just spoke. "Unless we're eating or screwing, my life is none of your business." She was trying hard to keep her sanity and *so* did not need mixed signals from him. He didn't get to act like he really cared—not that way. "Got it?"

He stood, towering over her even from several feet away. "That may be true, but no way am I going to let anybody harm the woman I'm fucking."

Fucking. Yeah, that's exactly what they were doing. She was so out of her depth, she'd lost sight of the shore miles ago. "Stay in your own compartment, Ryker. My business is my own, and you're not to get involved."

For the first time, anger sizzled across his features. "Be careful what you say, little girl. I'll make you eat those words."

She blinked. Sure, he'd been commanding in bed...a lot. But outside the bedroom, she'd never seen this side of him. "Don't threaten me."

"Then don't be obtuse. If you think I'm going to allow a man who hit you to keep walking, you've lost your damn mind." He put both hands on his fit hips, looking like a pissed-off warrior about to bellow a battle cry. "We may be casual, but even I have limits. A woman who cries on my shoulder after watching a stupid movie with dogs is someone who should never be harmed."

She gasped. "It wasn't stupid." It was sad when Juniper had died, darn it.

"Yeah. It was one of the dumbest movies ever made, and you turned into my shoulder to cry it out." He took a step toward her. "You don't want to mess with me on this. Trust me. Just give me the name, and tell me what's going on." Another step.

She couldn't back up any more or she'd be in the fireplace. So she held out a hand. Panic cramped her stomach, and she sucked in air and tried for anger. There it was. "I created a situation, there was an issue, and I've taken care of it." The truth would change his opinion, and she kind of enjoyed the view from the pedestal he temporarily had her on.

"No way did you create any situation that resulted in violence." The tone was almost mocking.

"That's it. You don't know me." Her chin lifted.

Something too dark to be amusement lifted his lips. "Oh, don't I?"

"No, you don't." Steam should be coming out of her ears. She reached down and plucked a high heel off. It was time to stop pretending to be somebody she just was *not*. "I don't like these, and I sure as shit don't walk around at work in them." Her tone was two octaves higher than normal, and she couldn't help it. Angling back, she threw the shoe at his head.

With lightning-quick reflexes, he grabbed the strap before the shoe took out his eye. "Zara." The tone was low and controlled…like always.

"You wouldn't like the real me." She kicked off the other shoe, her mind buzzing and her temper flying free. Reaching under her skirt, she yanked off the G-string underwear that had been shoved up her butt, her legs wobbling when she pulled them down and over her feet. "*Nobody* likes these." She flung it at his head. "I only wear them for you."

He snatched the flimsy material with one finger, his cheek creasing.

She fought the urge to stomp her foot and look like an idiot. He wasn't getting it. "I don't even know where you live," she yelled.

His phone buzzed, and he held up a hand. "Put the tantrum on hold, just for a second." Drawing the phone out, he read the screen. Both his eyebrows drew down, and he lifted the phone to his ear. "We've had movement?" Then he held still. His jaw hardened even more. "Damn it. Okay, I'm going." He paused, and his eyes darkened. "Because you just got shot. It's my turn to go, and I'll be right there." He shoved his phone back into his pocket.

Her breath heated. "Who got shot?"

"My brother."

Ryker had a brother?

He took several steps forward to grasp her neck.

She stilled. He'd never grabbed her neck before. Sure, his hold was gentle, but his hand was *wrapped around her neck*. "What are you doing?" she squeaked.

He leaned in, pressing just enough to show his strength. "I know you don't wear shoes like that at work, and I know the underwear set is just for me. I like that." He pressed a hard kiss to her mouth before drawing away. "I have to go, or I'd stay until we reached an agreement tonight. That bruise on your face offends me, and I'm done coddling you about it. You've got until tomorrow morning to give me the name of the guy who hit you, so I can have a conversation with him."

Ryker released her to grab his jacket and stride for the front door.

"Or what?" she asked, her voice trembling.

He opened the door and paused, looking back at her. "Or I'll find him myself and take him out for good." He yanked on his jacket, looking exactly like the badass rambling man he was. "And Zara? About where I live?"

"Yeah?"

"I moved permanently to Cisco a week ago."

On behalf of 1001 Dark Nights,

Liz Berry and M.J. Rose would like to thank ~

Steve Berry
Doug Scofield
Kim Guidroz
Jillian Stein
InkSlinger PR
Dan Slater
Asha Hossain
Chris Graham
Pamela Jamison
Fedora Chen
Jessica Johns
Dylan Stockton
Richard Blake
BookTrib After Dark
The Dinner Party Show
and Simon Lipskar

Made in the USA
Middletown, DE
21 March 2023

27277306R00080